Carved in Stone

© 2016 by Jen Silver

Affinity E-Book Press NZ LTD
Canterbury, New Zealand

1st Edition

ISBN: 978-0-908351-78-7

Editor: Angela Koenig
Proof Editor: Alexis Smith
Cover Design: Irish Dragon Designs

Acknowledgments

Thankful, as ever, to the fantastic Affinity team, always willing to give advice to a novice author. Every attention to detail is managed with care through editing, proofing, formatting and cover design.

Many thanks to JP for patiently answering my questions about police procedures. Any inaccuracies or misinterpretations are entirely my own.

And thank you, as always to my partner, Anne. Without her unfailing love and support, these stories wouldn't get written.

Carved in Stone

Starling Hill Trilogy
Book 3

Jen Silver

Carved in Stone

Starling Hill Trilogy
Book 3

Jen Silver

Affinity
eBook Press
NZ
2016

Dedication

For JP, a true friend who keeps me laughing, and can be counted on to lower the tone of any occasion.

Table of Contents

Also by Jen Silver

Starling Hill Trilogy
Starting Over
Arc Over Time
Carved in Stone

Short Stories
There Was a Time (Short Story)
The Christmas Sweepstake (Affinity's 2014 Christmas
Collection)

Author's Note

Of a Vaguely Historical Nature

Cartimandua was the leader of the Brigantes, the largest tribe in first century Britain. The Brigantes territory covered the northern half of the country now called England, from Cheshire up to Hadrian's Wall. Not much is known about this woman. She reigned during a time of great upheaval when the Roman legions returned to Britain in AD43, determined to add it to their empire. Cartimandua was unique amongst other tribal leaders of the time in deciding to cooperate with the invaders rather than see her people slaughtered. This didn't sit well with the man she married. Things came to a head when he openly opposed her policy and started an armed revolt against the invaders. She divorced him and took up with his armor bearer, Vellocatus.

Then she disappears from history. No one knows where she went once she was deposed and her remains have never been found. This made my job as a storyteller easier. I could make it up.

Through the characters in this story—and the previous two books, *Starting Over* and *Arc Over Time*—the location of Cartimandua's final resting place is discovered. An exhibition showcasing the finds from the site at Starling Hill farm in West Yorkshire is mounted at the British Museum. Now the queen lets it be known that she desires a proper reburial. She also wants a permanent monument to memorialize not just her place as an important historical figure, but also her love for the woman who remained by her side when she lost everything...position, home, wealth, power.

Two thousand years later—through the efforts of the modern day women in this story, all following their own paths to love and happiness—this dream can become a reality.

Carved in Stone is my attempt to give Queen Cartimandua a place in history worthy of a woman who reigned during a very difficult time and was vilified for trying to keep her people safe. May she and her lover finally rest in peace.

Prologue

A lot can happen in a year. Jo knew she had much to be thankful for in spite of being homeless and living off the generosity of friends. Homelessness wasn't an unusual state for her. She'd spent the last ten years drifting, living mostly out of her ancient camper van. It was a way of life she had been mostly happy with ever since leaving home and changing her surname from Johnson to Bright Flame.

She got by, making things and selling them at markets, fairs, and music festivals. Various girlfriends had come and gone but she now had a constant companion, Harry, the border collie she'd found abandoned at one of the festivals.

One of her one-night stands, Robin Fanshawe, was the reason she currently had a roof over her head. She'd spent an enjoyable summer on a craft barge moored near Hebden Bridge. Molly, the owner of the boat, was as much a drifter as she was, and she drifted off one day leaving Jo and Harry high and dry. Jo had been facing a winter in the van when Robin stopped by her market stall one morning and said she was welcome to come and stay at the farm.

The farm. Starling Hill farm, to be precise. The farm where it had all started the year before. During the night spent with Robin she had also learned that her partner was a potter. Jo had always fancied making pottery and took Robin at her word when she told her to stop by sometime.

One summer's day, driving up the long track to the farm nestled in the hills above Huddersfield, Jo had a sense of coming home.

That day turned out to be a catalyst of change for everyone there. Jo had bonded immediately with Eleanor Winters, the potter and owner of the farm. Eleanor, or Ellie as she preferred to be called, was happy to show her the pottery setup and didn't seem to mind about her brief encounter with Robin. There was another woman there though, who seemed to be more of a threat to Ellie's peace of mind; one Jasmine Pepper who had travelled up from London to spend time with Robin, whom she'd been seeing on and off for a few months.

Ellie's son and his girlfriend also arrived with the news that they were expecting a baby. And then, just as they were all sitting down for dinner together, another person came. This was Dr. Kathryn Moss, a one-time lover of Ellie's who, as an archaeologist, had an interest in digging up one of the fields on the farm.

The dig had been amazing. Initially, Dr. Moss, or "the professor," as Robin liked to call her, thought it would be a fairly routine field experience for her university students, excavating some Roman buildings. With the discovery of the royal burial site, it turned out to be so much more, bringing the farm and its occupants to the attention of worldwide media; mainly through the efforts of Jasmine and her journalist friend, Denise Sullivan.

Denise was totally smitten with the professor and Jo had spent time with her on the barge, only a few weeks ago, when she was wondering if her love would ever be reciprocated. The last she'd heard, Den had moved from London to Durham to be with Kathryn. Jo wondered how that was working out.

And it wasn't that long ago, May, that she had been a maid of honor at Ellie and Robin's wedding. She liked to think she had been instrumental in bringing them back together, through the upheaval of the dig and the unearthing of hidden treasures.

That summer's day she had driven up the farm track not knowing the changes that would be set in motion. Now things had come full circle and she was back at the farm. This time though, she was on her own, and in charge.

Part One

Awakenings

Chapter One

A world away from the valley and the noises she had grown used to over the months spent on the narrow boat, Jo had expected to enjoy the quiet of the farm. Used to waking to footsteps on the towpath, a dog being called to heel, a cyclist's bell, cars passing on the road above, at the farm there was nothing. She could have been in space, floating above the earth. As night settled over the farm and she lay down on the bed in a strange room, the eerie silence was unnerving. She started at every sound while Harry snored, his head resting comfortably on the other pillow.

"Some guard dog you are," she grumbled at him. Fleur, the smaller of the two cats was sleeping on the armchair in the corner. Soames, the ginger one, was roaming about outside. Ellie had assured her this was normal practice. She had also assured Jo that there were no foxes in the vicinity to bother the chickens.

It had seemed a good idea when Ellie asked if Jo would mind farm-sitting. Ellie and Robin were going to London for the opening of the exhibition at the British Museum featuring the royal bones and relics found at Starling Hill. The recent breakup with her girlfriend of seven months was still raw and she was keen to repay Ellie and Robin's generosity in offering her a roof over her head. Although now, in the early hours, she wondered what she had taken on.

Relief came at daybreak. She had only dozed on and off through the night. After completing the morning chores, releasing the chickens from their coop, collecting the eggs, replenishing food and water bowls for the dog and the cats, Jo thought she would set up the pottery wheel after breakfast and try her hand at creating a bowl or two.

The day passed slowly. The hills were bare with the onset of autumn. Harry was ecstatic running all over, sniffing everything, and marking out his territory at every blade of grass. After the months on the boat and only being taken for walks on a lead or the occasional park outing, this was doggy heaven. Jo was finding the freshness of the air almost too strong for her lungs, like being on a mountain.

Ellie's call woke her from an afternoon nap on the living room sofa.

"Everything okay?"

"Yes. No problem. Animals all fed and watered. Is it okay if I fire up the kiln?"

"Sure. You know how to use it. Just don't leave it on overnight."

"Right. How are things there?"

"Oh, good. The hotel's lovely, close to everything. I've been on the London Eye. It was a clear day and the views of the city from up there are amazing."

"You're braver than I am. I couldn't do it."

"Neither could Rob. She stayed on the ground and waved to me."

"Wow. Mega butch points lost there."

"I know. But I'm sure she'll make up for it in other ways."

"Just stop there, Ellie. Anyway, all the best for tonight."

"Thanks. Remember, no wild parties while we're away."

"As if. Take care. Love to Rob."

Jo fired her pots and made supper. Watched the sunset. Made sure the chickens were secure in their coop for the night. Still a lot of evening was left with nothing much on the telly. She tried strumming a few tunes on her guitar but she wasn't really in the mood. Harry seemed to sense her unease and kept resting his head on her knee, looking up at her face with big brown eyes.

Deciding she should stay up as long as possible to try and get a good night's sleep, she watched the ten o'clock news. There was a fairly restrained story on the exhibition, nothing too sensational. The Sappho of the North seemed to be the most popular phrase. Facebook and Twitter were already trending with "lezzie queen comes out of the closet" so there would likely be a more sensationalist tone in the tabloid press. She gave up scrolling through her timelines. Some comments were hysterical, some hilarious, and some just plain silly, although the homophobic trolls didn't seem to have picked up on it yet.

At eleven o'clock, jerking awake after dozing off in the chair, she told Harry they were going to bed and headed for the stairs. Once in bed, the sleep mode that had seemed inevitable in the living room eluded her. She thought about calling her friends in Hebden Bridge, Wade and Ian, to see if they would like to join her at the farm. She didn't know how Ellie coped on the nights when Robin was away, but then she had lived here most of her life. This lack of noise was normal to her.

She dozed off eventually only to be wakened a short time later. It was still very dark. The bedside clock showed 2:37 a.m. There were sounds outside, shuffling sounds, definitely not a cat, something much larger.

Finally, unable to stand it any longer, she dialed 999.

†

Ellie woke from the dream with a start. She had been alone in the museum with Queen Cartimandua. The queen was telling her she wanted to go home and where could she find a horse. The sound of a horse neighing woke her up. But there was no horse in the hotel bedroom, only Robin snoring lightly next to her.

Memories of the exhibition came back to her. The 3D reconstructions of the heads of Cartimandua and Vellocatus had been very lifelike, the queen's eyes seeming to bore into her. The images were very close to her own idea of the two women in her painting that was being used to advertise the exhibition. A painting she felt a particular affinity with. The queen's voice was clear in her head, *I want to go home.* But where was home? One of the Brigantes' strongholds or Starling Hill, Ellie's home, where her bones had been found?

She snuggled in closer to Robin's warm body. Ellie could understand the desire to find one's home that had surfaced through the dream. Her relationship with Robin had nearly come to an end when Kathryn reappeared in her life again. The dig on the farm laid bare not just centuries' old secrets, but her own deepest fears and insecurities. She had pushed Robin away, thinking that was the problem. But, of course, it wasn't. Life, without Robin in it, just wasn't any life at all. With all that had happened over the past year, they had finally come home, to each other.

Robin stirred beside her and reached over, placing a hand possessively on one breast. Ellie turned her head to see her lover looking at her, eyes wide with the grin on her face that meant only one thing. She smiled back. It was something she loved waking up to these days and she snuggled in close for the first kiss of the day. Robin's strong arms encircled her and dispelled the disturbing images of the night.

"What's the plan for today, hon?" she asked.

Robin's grin grew wider. "After I've ravished you, which may take some time, we'll venture out for coffee and make our way to Henry's. He promised us a slap-up brunch, remember?"

"I don't remember much from last night."

Hazel eyes burned into her as Robin moved a hand down past her navel. Finding the warmth and wetness already seeping out from between Ellie's thighs, she smirked knowingly. "Seems this part of you has remembered something."

Ellie arched up to meet Robin's searching fingers. Married for five months now and they were still making out like teenagers on steroids. She couldn't get enough of Robin's lovemaking and heard herself moan with desire for more as the probing digits found her clit already engorged.

†

Dr. Kathryn Moss woke to a clicking sound. It was early; the only light seemed to be coming from the streetlights through a gap in the curtains. She could just make out the form of her lover, Denise Sullivan, sitting in a chair hunched over her laptop. She was typing at a furious pace. Kathryn propped herself up on one elbow to watch her. Memories of the night before flooded back. Looking down at her hand, she could just make out the ring, a silver band inlaid with sapphires. She had become engaged last night.

There were the glasses of champagne on the table, mainly full. They had ignored the drink in favor of celebrating their new status with energetic lovemaking.

Den looked up and noticed she was awake. "You won't believe some of these idiots, Kat," she said, waving a free hand at the laptop screen. "Facebook pages already set up with hundreds of members…Cartimandua reigns, Vellocatus rocks, and my favorite so far, Sleek Ponies."

"They must be the academics." Sleek Pony was one of the most accepted translations of the queen's name.

Den laughed. "Yeah." She closed the laptop and walked over to the bed. "I didn't want to wake you." She leaned over and kissed Kathryn on the forehead.

Kathryn smiled up at her. It was hard to resist Den and the aroma rising from the bedclothes, evidence of their night of passion, was arousing her libido again.

†

It was after four in the morning before anyone arrived. Jo had got dressed and was on her second cup of strong coffee when the police car pulled up in the yard. She went out to meet them. However there was only one, a policewoman, who got out and reached back in to retrieve her hat. She put it on before approaching Jo.

"Hi. Sorry for the delay. We're a bit short staffed tonight and I had to wait for a car. PC Ashworth. What's the problem, ma'am?"

Jo stared. She must be getting old if an officer of the law who looked about fifteen was addressing her as ma'am.

"I was hearing noises. It sounded like there was someone here."

"I see. And you're on your own?"

"Just me and my dog who didn't wake up. Oh, plus two cats and the chickens."

"Okay. Well, I'll just take a look around." The policewoman opened the boot of her car and took out a large torch. "What's in the stables?"

"It's an art and pottery studio."

"Is it locked?"

"Are you kidding? Nothing gets locked around here."

"Of course." She flashed the beam of the torch around the yard and gave Jo an encouraging smile. "Do you want to come with me?"

With the tour of the buildings and the farmyard completed, Jo offered PC Ashworth a cup of tea or coffee. Sitting in the warmth of the farm kitchen, Jo could finally see that the officer was closer to her age than she originally thought. And with her hat off, her close-cropped hair looked to be a dusty blonde color, reminding Jo of the journalist, Den.

"I'm sorry to have brought you out here for nothing," she said, pushing the sugar bowl within reach.

"Happens all the time. Anyway, the boss thought it was worth a look. Starling Hill still raises a red flag from the trouble you had here last year."

"I suppose there might be renewed interest now that the exhibition's opened."

"What exhibition's that?"

Jo told her about the display now on at the British Museum.

PC Ashworth stirred her coffee thoughtfully. "Hm. Seems a bit of a long shot that anyone would want to come and look at an empty field, particularly in the middle of the night."

"Ellie's always been worried about treasure-hunters. Even though it's been made clear that nothing's left. All the artefacts of any value were uncovered and sent to the museum."

They sat in silence for a while. Harry was still asleep upstairs. The surfeit of fresh air and exercise had obviously worn him out.

"Is that your camper van?"

"Yes."

"Do you live in it?"

"On and off, when I'm homeless. Like now."

"What do you do?"

"I make things and sell them. I have a market stall on Wednesdays in Hebden Bridge. And until last week I was living on a canal boat. During the summer we were able to moor by the marina and advertise as a craft barge. Did extremely well with loom bands and sock puppets."

Whatever PC Ashworth made of that, Jo didn't find out as the officer's radio crackled. It was hard to make out what was being said but it brought an end to their conversation.

"Gotta go. Thanks for the coffee. If you hear anything else that worries you, don't hesitate to call." She picked up her hat and left, talking into her device as she went.

Jo sat for a while longer debating whether to go back to bed. But she'd had too much coffee. It was starting to get light, so she went outside to release the chickens and collect the eggs.

†

Steph stroked Jas's leg, soft and smooth to her touch. Waking up next to her lover's warmth was something she was still getting used to. Weekdays and most Saturdays she was up early, off to tend someone's garden before Jas was fully awake. But today was Sunday. A day made for loving. She let her hand wander up the leg to the tender part of the inner thigh. It was warmer here.

Jas let out a contented sigh and rolled towards her. Steph warmed to her task, letting her fingers trail through Jas's bush, the hint of moisture greeting her exploring fingers. The woman now opening beneath her moaned softly.

The taste of her lover as the warm juices flowed into her mouth spurred Steph on to use her tongue to great effect and Jasmine's hold on her hair as she bucked under her ministrations only increased the pressure she was able to exert with her mouth.

As Jas's orgasm subsided, Steph pulled herself up next to her and kissed her deeply. "I want to fuck you harder," she whispered hoarsely.

Another ecstatic moan from Jas told her this was a welcome idea but her next words put a damper on the whole morning.

"We'll need to get up soon," Jas said, idly tracing the outline of Steph's jaw. "Robin and Ellie are coming over for brunch."

"I don't know why Henry had to invite them here."

"He felt bad about Paul not being able to go to the exhibition last night. I guess he wanted to make up for that."

"Paul's going to the exhibition next week."

Jasmine sat up and looked into her eyes. "What's up? Don't you want to meet them? I would have introduced you properly last night, but I was busy with the media stuff."

"But it's not like you're really friends, is it? I didn't think you liked Ellie Winters. And as for that Robin, well…"

"That's it, isn't it? You're jealous. You think I still have a thing for Robin?"

Steph pulled away from her. "She is very good looking."

"Looks aren't everything."

"Oh, so you're saying I'm ugly."

"Steph! Stop it. You're everything I want and more. Robin's history. Ancient history." Jas licked her lips, seductively. "What do I have to do to prove that to you?"

"I think you have a very good idea," Steph gave her butt a gentle slap.

"Oh, you want to play, do you? That can be arranged."

Steph had to be satisfied with the promise of one of their favorite games later. For now, she was going to have to get up and be nice to the two women from the farm.

†

"Are you sure you know where you're going?" Ellie asked again.

Robin didn't answer, just kept hold of her hand and walked on. The green girders of a large bridge appeared and she turned to Ellie with a grin. "Of course. It's easy from here."

The tube journey from the hotel and the walk around the traffic system had been discouraging but the sight of the river lifted Ellie's spirits. Walking along by the rapidly moving water, Ellie was enchanted by everything.

"We should do this more often."

"Come to London?" Robin looked at her, eyebrows raised in surprise.

"No. I meant visit friends."

"Den's invited us to Durham."

They walked on in silence. It didn't need to be said. They both knew that wasn't likely to happen. Not if Kathryn was there.

"I thought Jas looked pretty happy last night," Ellie said as they passed yet another interesting looking pub.

Robin grunted.

Mention of ex-lovers was obviously not appreciated.

Wanting to dispel the change of mood, Ellie let go of her hand and moved closer to the wall. After a moment Robin joined her. They watched a lone kayaker paddle quickly past on the river, heading towards the bridge and the city beyond. Ellie put her arm around Robin's waist and pulled her close. "I love being here with you," she whispered.

Robin smiled then. "Me too." She kissed her lightly on the mouth. "Come on. They'll be sending out a search party."

"It was kind of them to invite us. But we hardly know them."

"Yeah, I know. It's a bit weird with Den not being here. But Henry seems like a nice guy. And Den says his boyfriend's a lot of fun too."

"She and Henry were close?"

"They still are, I think. Like brother and sister from what she's told me." Robin steered her away from the river. "This is the street. It's just along here."

A young man met them at the door of the smart-looking terraced house, greeting them enthusiastically. "Welcome. I'm Paul and I would have no trouble recognizing either of you from Henry's description. Come on in. Henry's in the kitchen. He's been cooking all morning."

"Really, he needn't have gone to any trouble," Ellie protested.

"Oh, he loves it."

They followed Paul down the dark hallway to the back of the house, emerging into a brightly lit kitchen that was the antithesis of the one at the farm. Gleaming stainless steel appliances, every modern convenience, completed by Henry wearing a spotless white apron and chef's hat. Several trays of delicious looking nibbles were spread across the counter.

Ellie couldn't help thinking what a handsome couple they were. Henry was tall, slim, dark haired—every inch the poster version of an airline pilot. Paul was shorter with neatly trimmed blond hair and wearing a t-shirt that emphasized his muscular physique. She knew that he was a ward nurse and had been working a shift the night before, which was why he hadn't been able to attend the exhibition with the others. That reminded her that the other housemates weren't there.

"Are Jasmine and her girlfriend joining us?" she asked.

"They're probably still in bed." Henry looked up from arranging the cheese platter and gave them a brilliant smile. "Steph works six days a week and enjoys a lie in on Sundays."

"Is that what you call it?"

"Paul! No need to embarrass our guests."

A loud thump came from above as if on cue.

"Ah. Well, I guess they're up. That'll be the lodgers in the shower." He turned to his partner. "Come on, Paulie, offer our guests something to drink and take them into the living room. I'll join you in a few." He bent down to look at something in the oven.

†

Den glanced out the window and realized that, as the flat landscape gave way to the northern hills, she was starting to feel like she was coming home. She had never thought she would be happy to move out of London, but after just a few weeks of living with the woman she loved, she couldn't imagine being anywhere else. The last few days had reminded her how crowded and noisy the big city was.

Sitting opposite her, Kathryn was reading an academic paper, looking very professor-like with her glasses perched on the end of her nose. Den loved watching her, and when Kathryn's fingers moved, the light glinted off the sapphires in the ring. Sometime during the night when their mouths weren't otherwise engaged, Kathryn had asked her where the ring came from. She didn't think Den could afford such a stunning piece of jewelry. She was right, of course. Den had confided in her mother, telling her she was going to ask Kathryn to marry her. After her mother got over the shock of Den committing herself to someone, she produced the ring, a family heirloom that she had wanted to pass on but feared her younger daughter would never need. It wouldn't have occurred naturally to Den to consider it, but after her conversation with Jo Bright Flame in the summer, she had looked up Kathryn's birth sign and discovered that sapphire was the stone associated with Virgos. It was no surprise to find that Virgo was an "earth" sign. She could almost believe the stuff, but some of the traits listed didn't fit at all with the professor's personality.

Den still couldn't quite believe she was now looking at her fiancée. Kathryn's commitment phobia had the journalist chasing her all over the country during the summer. Den had finally realized it was up to her to make the move. The long distance relationship just didn't work. Moving away from London was something she had never thought she would do, but if it meant having a life with Kathryn, she knew it was inevitable. Henry understood, as always. They had been friends from an early age and he'd helped her find her feet when she'd dropped out of university, much to her parents' disappointment. Henry not only offered her a room to rent in his newly purchased house, but gave her the push she needed to embark on her career in journalism. And if it weren't for Henry's recent interventions, she thought, she wouldn't be sitting across from the love of her life now.

Was Kathryn still in love with Ellie? She didn't want to believe it, their lovemaking that morning had been as sensationally fulfilling as ever, but with the train bringing them closer to the north and Ellie's home, she couldn't stop that thought from entering her mind. With all that had happened at Starling Hill farm, Ellie Winters would always be part of their lives.

The train stopped at York. Kathryn looked up from her paper as more passengers shuffled past looking for their reserved seats.

"You know, we were lucky to find any bones at all."

Den was used to such random comments from her lover, but this statement just confirmed how closely their lives were destined to be entangled with the farm and its owner.

"I mean, at Sutton Hoo they've only got an impression in the sand, the bones completely disintegrated. Acidic soil." Kathryn peered over her glasses.

"Preserved in sheep shit at Starling Hill."

"Crudely put, as usual. But, yes. I've never seen a site where there's not been a few centuries worth of disturbance. Farming, building…"

"Guess the remoteness of the landscape helped. And the anaerobic conditions."

Kathryn smiled at her. "Oh, you do read something other than trash."

Den didn't rise to the bait. When she'd unpacked her books at the flat, Kathryn had inspected her shelves and been dismissive of her collection of reading material.

"Anyway, Ed's having some more meetings on Monday with other bone specialists."

Dr. Ed McLaughlin was a former colleague of Kathryn's and had been closely involved with the dig at

Starling Hill. He specialized in osteoarchaeology, and his expertise had played a big part in making sure the bones were properly excavated and preserved.

"Why? What's going on, Kat?" Den's journalistic nose was twitching.

"The bones weren't the only things that were intact."

"Come on, Professor. Give. This is like pulling teeth."

Kathryn smiled broadly. "Got it in one. The teeth."

"So?"

"So, follow it through, Sherlock."

Den closed her eyes. The train had picked up speed since leaving York behind. They were getting close to their final destination, the medieval city of Durham with its crumbling castle and magnificent cathedral. And now their home since Kathryn had taken up a position in the university's archaeology department.

Her eyes snapped open as the answer came to her. "No way! Two thousand years. You won't find any matches now, surely."

"Don't call me Shirley! But, you never know, do you? They were finding Richard's relatives all over the world, Canada, New Zealand."

She was referring to the discovery of Richard III's skeleton two years before. The mitochondrial DNA preserved in the teeth had meant that it could be proved beyond doubt that the bones were those of the last Plantagenet king.

"But they already had genealogy records to back up the theory. No one can go back much further than five hundred years. There certainly aren't any records for the first century. We don't even know Cartimandua's last name. Brigantes territory comprised most of northern England. Which has been over-run by how many different invaders?"

"People are happy to pay to have their DNA tested. The project will fund itself, and someone, somewhere, will be a match."

"Bit of a lottery."

"Yes, but who wouldn't want to find out if they're related to the queen who ruled over the largest tribe in Britain?"

"Not everyone thinks Cartimandua was such a great ruler. They'd rather be connected to Boudica."

"Ha! Not everyone thinks Boudica was a real person. She could be as much of a myth as King Arthur and Robin Hood."

"And why are you telling me this?" Den didn't really need to ask but she wanted to hear Kathryn say it.

"Because, once we get the go-ahead, we'll need to publicize the project. And you can tell a great story."

†

Henry wondered if his hosting skills had lost their edge. He was finding it difficult to keep a conversation going with Ellie. The ethereal quality he had noticed the night before at the museum seemed even more pronounced in the light of day. Robin had disappeared into the kitchen to get more food and Jasmine was telling Paul about all the posts now on Facebook with different fan groups springing up for the queen and her consort.

"So, uh, I gather you don't do much pottery nowadays."

Ellie looked at him, appearing to come back from somewhere far away. "No."

"That painting of yours, the one they've used on the posters for the exhibition, it's amazing. The scene is so evocative. Did you paint it from memory or a photograph?"

"It's where we live. That's what it looks like." She smiled at Henry and he felt a warmth spread throughout his body. "You'll have to come and visit."

"Yes, we'd like that. When we manage to have holidays together, we usually go somewhere in this country. I hate being a passenger on a plane even for short flights. Anyway, our favorite destinations are generally Devon or Cornwall. Guess we're due a trip up to the wilds of Yorkshire. Den's been after us to visit Durham as well."

"Yes. The weather's likely to be crap, but the scenery makes up for it. Part of the charm, if you can call it that."

Paul and Jasmine had stopped talking and were listening to them now.

Ellie looked over at them. "You're more than welcome to visit any time."

"That would be awesome," Paul chimed in. "I would love to see the site."

"It's all been covered over now. Just one bit of Roman wall left to see. We mostly use it to sit on in the summer."

Jas looked around. "Where's Steph gone?"

"I think she went to get another drink." Henry gave the glasses on the table a glance. "Does anyone else want more?"

"No, I'm fine, thanks." Ellie had barely touched her wine.

Paul got up and topped up everyone else's glasses from the bottle. "It's a shame Den and Kathryn couldn't have joined us today."

"Well, they were catching a morning train back up north. I wonder how the proposal went?"

"Proposal?"

"Yeah, Den was planning to propose to Kathryn last night. I told her it's too soon." Henry took a sip of his wine. "But since I haven't had an anguished text message from her, the professor must've have said 'yes'."

"I don't believe it. Our Den getting married!" Paul laughed.

"I don't believe it, either," Ellie said. They all looked at her. "Not about Den. I'm sure it's what she wants. But, Kathryn, well…"

"That's what I tried to tell her, but she won't listen to me."

Jasmine excused herself. "I think I'll see what Steph's up to."

After she left, Henry laughed. "It'll be those two next. Honestly, lesbians!"

"Aren't you two going to tie the knot?" Ellie asked, looking from one to the other.

Paul shook his head, sadly. "He hasn't asked me. I'm going to wait for a leap year, then I'll ask him."

"Actually we're still arguing about who will wear the frock."

Ellie laughed when she realized she was being teased. She drank some of her wine and Henry was glad to see she was finally relaxing with them.

†

Robin could feel the other woman's eyes on her as she helped herself to another elegant creation of smoked salmon and cream cheese delicately poised on a small fish-shaped cracker. None of this food would have looked out of place at the Queen's annual garden party.

"Fantastic spread. You must love living here." She glanced over to where Steph was leaning against the doorframe. Their eyes met for a second before they both looked away. Robin debated whether or not to take Ellie a cucumber and egg sandwich. She had hardly touched any food, and seemed preoccupied.

"How long did you and Jas know each other?"

Robin heard the hostility in the woman's tone. She placed two of the beautifully crafted crust-less sandwiches on her plate. "Not long. Six or seven months, on and off."

"So, you just used her for a good screw when you felt like it."

Putting the plate carefully on the counter, Robin turned around. "Look, Stella…"

"Steph."

"Whatever. It was never a serious commitment for either of us."

"Jasmine thought so. She was in love with you."

"Well, I wasn't in love with her. So get over it."

If she hadn't been watching for it, Steph would have easily landed a blow on her nose. As it was, the boxing sessions paid off and she ducked in time, and then caught the gardener off balance by head-butting her in the stomach. Steph fell back against the counter.

"Oh, shit. Are you all right?"

Steph's eyelids flicked open and the brown eyes had lost something of their malevolent stare. "Fuck off."

Robin smiled at her and to her surprise Steph smiled back. She pulled herself upright and seated herself on a stool.

"Are you really okay?"

"Yeah." Steph rubbed her side. "Might have a bit of a bruise later."

"So, how long have you and Jas been together?"

"About three months."

"Why did she pack her job in?"

"Oh, she got involved with someone she shouldn't have, a client. When that went pear-shaped, the client pulled the contract with her PR company, Armadillo. Jas said she'd been thinking about leaving before then anyway."

"How did you two meet?" The Jasmine Pepper Robin knew was always impeccably dressed. She'd even turned up at the farm the year before wearing designer clothes and high heels. Steph just didn't seem like her type.

"At a club. This client was coming on a bit heavy-handed. I just helped her out."

"Sounds like a bit of a mess." Robin assumed there was more to the story, but she wasn't going to ask.

"Yeah, well, it's fine now. She's happy. With me."

"Okay. I got that."

Steph was dressed casually in jeans and a tight-fitting, button-down shirt, but the leather belt was metal-studded and Robin hadn't missed the protective hold she had on Jas when they met briefly at the exhibition. Steph was shorter and stockier but Robin had no doubt she could be handy in a fight.

Jasmine arrived in the kitchen and immediately went over to Steph, kissing her on the cheek before asking, "You two okay in here?"

Robin picked up the plate of sandwiches and headed for the doorway. "Yeah, great. Just stocking up on goodies. Nice talking to you, Steph."

She could hear the murmur of their voices as she walked down the hall back to the living room. Robin smiled to herself. Steph wasn't likely to admit she'd been so easily knocked down. She had to admit that Jas was looking happier and more relaxed than she'd ever seen her. So, the gardener was obviously able to do something right.

†

Sorting through the debris of her life as she cleaned out the van, Jo considered what she had to show for her nearly forty years. A decrepit vehicle, a rescue dog, some pottery and other handmade crafts, memories of various music festivals, and assorted ex-girlfriends.

Once upon a time she'd had an actual job, but the world of work had moved on since then. She wouldn't know how to conform to an office environment nowadays. And she didn't want to. The thought of signing on at a job center and retraining filled her with dread.

When had she been happiest? She realized it was probably the year before, the summer of the dig. Those few weeks when she and Robin had shared a house, when she was housesitting for Wade and Ian while they were adventuring in Canada. Robin and Ellie finally managed their reconciliation and she had started a brief affair with Tina, one of the university students taking part in the dig, whose parents had thrown her out of the house after discovering her stash of lesbian reading material. The house in Hebden Bridge had provided an ideal refuge. Jo had been happy to take Tina under her wing, showing her how to make things and letting her help out on the market stall. It was news to her when Robin informed her the girl had developed a massive crush on her. Jo had been flattered but knew it wouldn't last. Tina only needed a helping hand, so to speak, to be initiated into lesbian sex. Jo viewed it as a public service and wasn't surprised or disappointed when their relationship ended once the new university term got underway. Tina reconciled with her parents but, having had a taste of freedom she had moved into student accommodation, made new friends, and was now living in a house share.

Then Jo met Molly just at the time when Wade and Ian were returning home, so the move to the barge had come at the right moment. Perhaps she and Molly could have worked things out but the cramped space of the narrow boat just seemed to exacerbate any minor frictions.

There was plenty of space at the farm but Jo did worry she might be outstaying her welcome. Robin and Ellie hadn't given any signs that they wanted her to move on, but she felt sometimes her presence was an imposition.

She shook her head to clear her mind. Too much time on her own, too much time to think negative thoughts.

Chapter Two

Robin looked up at the glass-fronted building and wondered if this would be a big waste of time. Her experience of working with corporate clients had never been happy. They paid well and usually on time. Even so, the working relationships weren't as satisfactory as with the smaller businesses where she could get a feel for the people, not just the product.

She gave her name to the heavily made-up stick insect sitting behind a massive reception desk and checked her over while the receptionist wrote out a name badge. The girl hardly looked old enough to be out of school without permission.

The molded plastic seats were uncomfortable so she stood by the glass doors and watched the traffic. It wasn't too late to cut and run. Ellie had said she was going back to the museum this morning. The exhibition was fully booked but Ed McLaughlin had given her a special pass. They had agreed to rendezvous back at the hotel after Robin's meeting and then go somewhere for lunch. It was a bit breezy, however Robin was hoping to convince Ellie to take a boat ride down the Thames to Greenwich afterwards.

"Robin Fanshawe?"

She turned to see a tall, willowy blonde with big tits approaching.

"Yes."

"Super! I'm Roisin, Max's PA."

"That's a nice name." Robin held onto her hand for longer than necessary.

"My grandparents were Irish, but they emigrated to Australia." She smiled at her as they walked towards the lift.

"Have you been here long?"

"Two years now. I'm getting married next year."

"Oh, great." Robin turned to look at the view as the lift ascended on the outside of the building, then quickly looked back when they passed the second floor. She'd managed to avoid going on the London Eye. This was worse. She concentrated on Roisin's most prominent features instead.

"Who's the lucky guy?" Robin asked when she managed to raise her eyes to the woman's face.

Roisin met her gaze easily. "Woman."

"Okay. Lucky woman, then?"

The lift stopped and Roisin gestured for her to get out first. Robin guessed she wasn't going to be given an answer.

Not that it mattered. Depending on the outcome of this meeting, she might never see her again. Engaging in a little mild flirtation was done more from habit than any actual interest.

Robin followed the PA through a well-appointed reception area. The seats looked much more comfortable than the ones in the lobby downstairs. The boardroom Roisin led her into had the appearance of any other she'd been in— long table, chairs on either side, one at the far end, large whiteboard screen at the other. There were no external windows, no distracting view of the ever-rising London skyline. If there had been a window, she was sure they would be on a level with the Shard, now the city's tallest building.

Roisin indicated which chair she should take, to the right of the one at the head of the table, and asked if she would like a coffee or tea.

"Coffee, please. Black, no sugar."

The buxom Aussie returned a few minutes later with a tray holding three cups. Coffee in teacups always looked anemic, Robin thought, and this reflection was borne out when Roisin placed a cup and saucer in front of her. She should have asked for milk, it might have given the drink some added substance.

Roisin sat down opposite. "Max won't be long. She's just finishing a call."

Swallowing a mouthful of the liquid from the cup, Robin concentrated on not showing her disgust at the lack of taste. "Fine."

"Coffee okay?"

"Yeah."

"No, it's not."

"Why do you give it to people then?"

"It's how Max likes it."

Any further discussion of the coffee and her boss's tastes was interrupted when the door opened and another woman entered—evidently the boss, Max Fleetwood. Power suit, power haircut, and power attitude. She sat down at the head of the table and started without introductions.

"Thank you for coming in, Ms. Fanshawe. Roisin, the brief."

Roisin handed Robin a neatly typed single sheet of paper. She glanced through it.

"I'm not sure why you wanted to see me. I don't do PR. You'd be better off with a company like Armadillo."

"We fired Armadillo."

"I know one of the account managers there. Jasmine Pepper. She has a good rep."

"Ah, we couldn't work with them. Their proposal looked fine on paper but it turned out we had a conflict of interest."

Robin caught the look that passed between Max and Roisin. Something Den had said surfaced in her mind. Jas packed her job in suddenly and moved in with Steph shortly after. She remembered Den telling her about switching rooms with Steph so that the new couple could enjoy the larger top floor space. Den was relocating to be with Kathryn in Durham and had only wanted the room to crash in at Henry's now and again whenever she had a London-based assignment. Robin's thoughts flashed on the aggressive posturing of the gardener the day before, her overly protective attitude towards Jas.

She looked at Max Fleetwood again. The woman's arrogant tone was annoying, as was the way her assistant fawned over her. Was this the client Jas got involved with? If so, Robin should have thanked Steph for whatever part she played in rescuing her.

"Graphics, web design, that's what I do."

"We think you have the skills to do the job. At least think about it."

"Sure." Robin just wanted to get out of the room now to clear her head. No way would she be working with this woman. She recognized a player when she saw one, and this one was well out of her league. After shaking hands and saying she could make her own way out, Robin kept her eyes closed on the way down the side of the building in the lift. There had to be another way to fund Ellie's dream journey on the Golden Eagle. One thing was certain; she didn't want to work for that woman.

Safe on the ground again, she checked the time on her phone. Time enough to walk the mile or so back to the hotel to meet Ellie. Time to get a decent cup of coffee somewhere as well. The meeting had left a bad taste in her mouth that she couldn't blame entirely on the coffee.

†

Monday mornings were so much better now. Jasmine couldn't believe how much her life had changed in such a short time. Steph was a big part of the change, of course. But leaving her job at Armadillo was the main reason she could now face Mondays without feeling a heavy weight on her chest.

She had gone back to sleep after Steph left to go to work, rolling over into the warm spot in the bed where her lover's body had been. Awake again with the light streaming in through the blinds, she was ready to get up and start her new morning routine of exercises, shower, coffee and a healthy bowl of muesli.

Deciding what to wear was also a lot easier now. She worked from home on her laptop most days and only had to dress up if she needed to meet a client. Still, she didn't like to look a total slob in front of the boys, so she put on a pair of tailored chinos and a maroon sweater that Steph told her went well with her eyes. Picking up the clothes discarded on the floor from the night before she discovered the dildo and harness nestled in a pair of her lover's shorts. It was unusual for Steph to leave it there. She was normally fastidious about cleaning their sex toys after use, but she'd been distracted last night.

Jasmine removed the dildo from the harness and took both items down to the bathroom to wash them. As she was putting them away memories of the day before came back to her. She had been talking to Paul in the living room when she suddenly realized Steph had been gone for longer than was necessary to fetch another beer. The standoff scene in the kitchen had struck her as comical, however they were both on their feet and there was no blood on the floor. She recognized Steph's pose from the times they'd been out clubbing. Robin was feigning her "couldn't care less" stance, leaning casually against the counter.

Seeing Robin again had been easier than she'd thought. At the exhibition Jasmine was preoccupied with the job Den had given her, tracking the social media sites and checking that the newspapers were honoring the press embargo on the release she'd sent out.

She hadn't been lying to Steph when she said she was over Robin. The unfortunate fling with Max Fleetwood had knocked that out of her. The happiness she had since found with Steph was real and sometimes she had to pinch herself to know it wasn't a dream. Introducing Steph to her parents, uncomfortable as it had been, released something in her she hadn't even realized she'd been holding back. Finally, for the first time in her life, approaching her forty-seventh birthday, she was free to be herself. Not just with certain friends, like Denise Sullivan, but with everyone. So more than one good thing had come out of her brief association with Max, she had also freed up desires she'd been hiding from herself all those years.

When she entered the kitchen, she walked over to Steph and kissed her lightly on the cheek. Not because she wanted to prove something to either her ex-lover or her current one, but because it felt like the natural thing to do. She was in love, truly in love, for the first time and an army of ex-lovers turning up for brunch wasn't going to change that.

Jas tucked the dildo and harness into their resting place in the bottom drawer of the dresser and headed downstairs with confidence, ready to face the day and whatever challenges it might bring.

†

It wasn't like Ellie to keep her waiting. She was normally obsessively early for everything. When half an hour passed without her showing up, Robin started to worry. No message had been left at reception. Ellie's phone, if she even had it with her, wasn't switched on. If she were still at the museum, Robin would need a pass to get into the exhibition. She couldn't just turn up and expect them to let her in. There was only one thing for it; she would have to phone the one person who could help.

†

Kathryn sipped at her coffee watching the river flow past. She only had to go in for a meeting at the university later. It was good to have the morning at home. The weekend had been emotionally draining. First, with the opening of the exhibition, she'd felt she was as much on show as the queen and her consort, and then with getting engaged. She twisted the ring on her finger. She'd only been wearing it for thirty-six hours and fiddling with it had already become a habit.

"Hey, Kat." Den's voice reached her from the kitchen. She didn't like the nickname when other people used it, but for some reason didn't mind it from Den. Her lover appeared in the doorway waving her mobile. "It's Robin. She wants to speak to you."

Kathryn raised her eyebrows. Robin was usually hostile towards her and unlikely to initiate a conversation. It hadn't escaped her notice that she'd been sticking to Ellie like glue at the exhibition opening.

"Something about Ellie."

She took the phone from Den's outstretched hand. "Hi."

Robin didn't waste time with pleasantries. "Ellie's at the exhibition. She was supposed to meet me an hour ago. I need to get in and find her. Can you help?"

"I think Ed's still there. Hang on, I'll call him from my phone." Kathryn retrieved her own mobile from the bag by the door. Ed answered right away telling her she was lucky to catch him between meetings. But she was able to get back to Robin with good news.

"He'll arrange for a pass to be left for you at the ticket desk. He would have gone in to look for Ellie himself, but he's tied up with another meeting now."

"Great. Thanks." Then she was gone.

Kathryn gave Den her phone back. "I guess she's grateful."

"She's just worried. They're still acting like newlyweds."

"They've known each other for twenty years. You would think they were past that stage."

Den pulled her close and kissed her lightly on the lips. "When you're in love, I don't think you ever get past that stage."

Kathryn let herself relax into Den's embrace. Was she in love? Or was it still lust? She was having trouble with the commitment concept. Engagement, fiancée, marriage. None of these words had featured in her life plan until now when the journalist had caught her by surprise, popping the question while she was still on an emotionally charged high from the success of the Cartimandua exhibition.

†

Robin marched up to the desk and waited impatiently for the man in front of her to finish asking questions about which galleries he should visit, and in which order. Once he'd gone off with his map, she identified herself.

"Robin Fanshawe. Dr. McLaughlin said he would leave a pass here for me to get into the Cartimandua exhibition."

"Oh, yes. Of course." The woman reached into a drawer and brought out a ticket—a yellow sticker attached with her name printed on it. "Do you know where to go?"

Considering there were big signs everywhere, Robin thought she could hardly miss it, but she decided against a snarky answer. "Yes, thanks. I was here for the opening."

"Oh. Is it as good as everyone says? I haven't had a chance to see it yet."

"Yes, it's amazing." She gave the woman a friendly smile and walked away.

Inside the gallery, she waited a moment to let her eyes adjust to the darkened interior. There was a large crowd gathered around the heads. Ellie must have been one of the first visitors to arrive. Robin could see her, seemingly oblivious to anyone else, standing directly in front of the reconstructed face of Queen Cartimandua.

A few people moved off to look at another exhibit and Robin was able to get through to Ellie without having to push anyone aside. Only when she got there did she realize that Ellie's eyes were closed. She glanced at the queen. The modeler had given her a haughty look. It wasn't a kind face. But then she had lived in difficult times, and being the leader of the largest tribe in Britain wouldn't have been easy for anyone, male or female, in the first century.

Ellie's eyes flicked open and she turned to Robin. "Hi, sweetie."

Robin swallowed back the emotional response that had been building for the last hour. "How did you know I was here?"

"The queen told me."

"The queen…" Robin looked at the 3D model again. It stared back imperiously.

"Is it lunchtime?"

"Yes." Robin grasped her hand. It was cold. "Come on, love."

Ellie didn't resist as she pulled her out of the crowd and out through the gallery doors. Once in the large atrium, Robin breathed a sigh of relief. Inside the gallery she'd felt as if the air was pressing down on her.

†

"Rob, I'm so sorry. I really didn't realize what time it was."

They were sitting in their hotel room, the remains of a room service sandwich mostly uneaten on the plate in front of her. Ellie stared at the back of Robin's head.

Robin turned away from the window. "I think we should go home today." She hadn't touched much of her lunch either.

"But, I thought you wanted to go down the river. Take a look at the Cutty Sark."

"The weather's not that great. We can go another time."

Ellie was troubled by the look on Robin's face. She had been in too much of a daze when Robin turned up at the museum to notice her partner's agitation. Instead of going to a restaurant as they'd agreed when they parted after

44

breakfast, Robin wanted to come back to the hotel. It had taken Ellie a while to notice how upset she was. When she finally asked her how the meeting went, Robin just shrugged and said it was a bust. Nothing else.

"Well, if that's what you really want, I don't mind."

"Okay, good."

Decision made, Robin leapt into action. She raced around, throwing clothes into the suitcase, taking a bit more time to make sure she had all the electronic devices and chargers stored in her backpack.

"You do the toiletries, El. I'll ring reception to let them know so they can have the bill ready for us and order a taxi."

There wasn't much left to pack. Ellie folded up the few things she'd hung in the wardrobe and checked the drawers for any stray socks or knickers. While she was in the bathroom, she could hear Robin on the phone. It sounded like she was talking to Jo. Ellie was happy to be going home. There was a picture forming in her mind, a picture that wanted to be painted.

†

Jo had kept herself busy all day Sunday and taken Harry for extra-long walks to tire herself out. During the evening her thoughts kept going back to the policewoman. Having grown up on army bases, she wasn't usually attracted to uniforms. They didn't have the same magnetic appeal as they did for many women. But something about PC

45

Ashworth's manner had attracted her. She was tempted to make another call-out during the night but decided against it—knowing her luck, it would be another cop who responded.

The call from Robin on Monday afternoon cheered Jo immensely. She was relieved they were coming home earlier than planned. Another night of listening to the silence, knowing there wasn't another person within a mile of the place, would have been hard.

Watching her two friends when they arrived back at the farm, Jo wondered what had happened. They seemed out of sorts with each other. Robin had taken off on her motorbike after dumping their suitcase and her backpack in the living room. Ellie had given Jo a brief smile and said she had something she wanted to do in the studio.

Wonderful. Now she was alone again. After making up the fire to get a good blaze, she settled down to read. Harry made himself comfortable on the couch next to her while the cats occupied Ellie's armchair. Even while she had the house to herself she hadn't used the chair. It was very much Ellie's space.

The sound of the bike brought Jo out of her reverie. She realized she hadn't read more than a few pages of her book in the last hour. It was one of Ellie's history books and maybe not the best thing to keep her attention for long.

Robin appeared, nodded to her and, picking up the suitcase, headed upstairs. A few minutes later Jo heard the shower running. She looked back at the book. It was no good, she couldn't concentrate on finding out how the sudden withdrawal of the Roman troops from Britain affected the native tribes. She knew that it led to the rise of the mythical King Arthur and that's what she really wanted to read about. It didn't look like this serious tome was going to give her much romance in the way of the stories about Camelot, the Round Table, and the whole love triangle with Arthur, Guinevere and Lancelot.

When Robin came back downstairs, Jo was staring into the fire and thinking about putting another log on.

"I'm going to get a beer. Do you want anything?" Robin asked from the doorway.

"Yeah. A beer would be great."

Robin came back with two bottles of Corona and placed them on the table. She then found her backpack and pulled her iPad out. Harry wasn't pleased to be disturbed, but he moved over when Robin gave him a gentle shove to let him know she wanted to sit next to Jo.

"Got some photos. Do you want to see them?"

"Sure." Jo put the book down and picked up a bottle. She enjoyed a long swallow of beer, while Robin located the pictures.

There were the usual tourist shots of places in London: Ellie outside Buckingham Palace next to an unsmiling guard, Ellie getting on the London Eye, pictures of the river, a couple of close-up selfies of the two of them. They looked happy and relaxed.

"Do you have any of the exhibition?"

"I couldn't take any as they don't allow it in the gallery. But Den sent me some of the publicity ones." Robin scrolled through her photos and found them. There was one of the two skeletons in their glass cases, and several of the 3D reconstructions of the heads taken from different angles.

"Wow. That's amazing. So lifelike. They look like they could talk."

"Yeah." Robin sighed, and closed the app. She put the iPad down and picked up her beer.

"What's going on with you two? You look really happy in those photos."

Robin sighed again. She stroked Fleur who had woken up when she sat down and decided to take the opportunity to sit on her lap. Soames had opened one eye briefly, stretched out when Fleur's absence afforded him more space, and gone back to sleep.

"I'm worried about Ellie."

Jo waited.

"This morning she returned to the gallery. It was what we'd planned. Ed had given her a pass. I had a meeting with a prospective client so we arranged to meet at twelve back at the hotel." Robin described how worried she'd been waiting for her, pacing back and forth in reception, checking her phone every few minutes for messages. She told Jo about having to contact Kathryn, getting a pass arranged for herself, and then finding Ellie standing in front of the queen.

"She was in a trance, Jo. But when I turned up, she opened her eyes. She said Cartimandua told her I was there.

And then she spent most of the train journey sketching something in her notepad."

"Awesome. She could be channeling the queen."

"Don't you think it's a bit scary? She's obsessed."

"You're jealous." Jo laughed.

"Of a two-thousand-year-old skeleton. Yeah, right."

"Well, you are. What was she drawing?"

"I don't know. It just looked like a field. Could be somewhere around here, like a lot of her paintings."

†

Ellie looked at the outline on the canvas. It was as she imagined it. No, that was wrong. It was as the queen described it. She stretched and glanced at her watch. It was much later than she expected. Her stomach rumbled. She hadn't eaten anything since the tuna baguette they'd shared on the train. Robin had bought it before they got on, saying they wouldn't get anything decent from the buffet car.

Robin. She really needed to talk to her. But how could she explain what was going on in her head without sounding like a nutcase?

Satisfied now she had the preliminary sketch done, she could apply the colors in the morning. She walked across the yard to the house and was charmed by the cozy scene. The fire, Jo and Robin, the cats, Harry. They all looked settled and warm. She was chilled to the bone.

"Hi. Do you guys want anything to eat?"

They both looked at her, startled. Had they been talking about her?

"I thought of putting together some cheese and crackers. And a glass of red wine. More beer?"

"Yeah, sure. I'll get them." Robin followed her into the kitchen.

They worked together in silence. Ellie put crackers and cheese out on the wooden cutting board. Robin got plates and knives together and some strips of kitchen roll to serve as napkins. She took two more bottles of Corona from the fridge, sliced the lime to put in the necks. Ellie poured her wine.

"Rob."

Robin turned, her eyes betraying the concern she'd held all day.

"I'm sorry. I can't really explain what's going on. It's just I have this strong sense of connection. I...I need you to hold me. To feel grounded again."

Her lover closed the gap between them quickly and embraced her. She stroked her hair. "Oh, God, Ellie. I was scared."

Ellie immediately felt warmed by Robin's closeness, her anchor to the real world. After a few minutes, she pulled away. "We better go back in before Jo thinks we've abandoned her." She kissed Robin lightly on the lips. "It will be okay. As long as I know you're here for me."

"Always."

†

Later that night, after they made love, and Ellie fell into a deep sleep, Robin lay awake wondering if she could keep that promise. More than anything she wanted to protect her love from harm. But how could she deal with something she couldn't see? Was Ellie losing her mind? Ellie's mother hadn't been much older when she first showed signs of dementia.

Robin breathed in the scent of Ellie's skin and wanted to touch her, to reassure herself that she was there, that she wasn't losing her. She drew her hand back, sighed and rolled over. The queen spoke to Ellie in her dreams as well. Was she just jealous, as Jo suggested? She wanted to understand, she really did. Maybe, given time, Cartimandua's presence in her head would fade and Ellie would return to normal. With another deep sigh, Robin let that thought comfort her as she drifted into an uneasy sleep.

Chapter Three

Market day, and Jo wondered why she was bothering to stand behind her stall getting cold. Not many visitors. It was wet and windy. Half the regular stallholders hadn't turned up as well.

Fergus on the clothes stall next to her came over and made a show of looking through her craft display. "How much do you want for these coasters?"

"There's a price on them."

"Sure, but we have to haggle, right."

"British people don't haggle. That's the price. Take it or leave it."

"Ooh. Who stepped on your corns this morning?"

"Fuck off, Ferg," she said, amicably. "You've got a customer."

He scuttled back to his stall and started a conversation with the person who had stopped to look at his selection of combat trousers. "Great weather for ducks," she heard him say.

Jo put the coasters back in their place. She was pleased how they had turned out. Old CD sleeves, cut to size and laminated on a solid cork backing. She'd already sold six sets.

"Hi. Nice weather for ducks."

She looked up to see if it was another stallholder come over to relieve the boredom and take the piss. The woman staring at her looked familiar but she couldn't place her from any of her known customers.

"Do I know you?"

"We met at Starling Hill a few nights ago. But you might not recognize me without the truncheon."

Jo smiled. The policewoman, out of uniform.

"Oh, of course. Sorry, I really didn't…without the…you know." Jo could feel herself blushing. "Is it a day off or are you working undercover? I have nothing to hide, officer."

"Day off. Just out for a bike ride."

Jo realized then that PC Ashworth was wearing lycra and holding a cycling helmet in one hand. An excellent disguise. She wouldn't have known her if she'd passed her in the street. The clear blue eyes were giving her the once over.

"You look like you could do with a break. Care to join me for coffee?"

"Um, yeah, that would be great. Not much happening here today." She called over to the next stall. "Hey Fergie! I'm taking some time out. Watch the stall and the coasters are yours."

He gave her the thumbs up. She collected her bag from under the table and walked around to join PC Ashworth.

They went into the cafe across from the market. It was generally always busy but today there was no problem getting a table in the corner by the window. The policewoman glanced around. "Seems like a friendly place."

"Yeah, I love it here."

Once their cappuccinos had been ordered, Jo looked at the woman seated across from her. "So, you know my name, but I don't want to keep calling you PC Ashworth."

"No, I guess not. My first name's Fiona, but only my mother uses that. Everyone else calls me Ash."

"Well, nice to meet you, Ash. What brings you to Hebden Bridge on a wet autumn day?"

"Like I said, just out for a ride."

Their coffees arrived. Ash took some of the froth off the top and licked it off her spoon. She caught Jo staring and smiled. "It's a bit of a commute for you from the farm."

"Yes. I'm looking for somewhere in town. But I'll have to get a proper job to be able to afford a place. And not everywhere is dog friendly."

"Ah yes, the enthusiastic guard dog."

"You haven't met Harry, have you? He loves it at the farm. But I know we can't stay there forever. Do you have any pets?"

"Not at the moment. My last girlfriend took the parrot with her."

Jo was going to ask if she missed the parrot, but she stopped herself in time, catching the twitch of the lips and raised eyebrows. It seemed Ash was subtly letting her know that she was a lesbian and she was available.

†

Robin watched the black and white dog streak excitedly around the field. She called to him and he made his way back, stopping to sniff interesting tufts of grass and occasionally lifting his leg. She knew how he felt although she didn't feel the need to pee on anything to stake a claim. Two days back at the farm and the time in London was fading into a distant memory. She enjoyed the bustle of the city when she was there, but the peace of the farm was what she loved.

Ellie was in the studio engrossed in her new painting. She hadn't been any less loving than usual but Robin felt her mind was somewhere else at times. Her hope that Ellie's obsession with the queen would dissipate as she got back into her daily routine had been shattered with the arrival of a parcel. The sight of a Royal Mail van struggling up the lane was an unusual sight. Robin was returning from the chicken run with the eggs when it arrived on Wednesday morning.

She signed for the large recorded delivery package and took it into the studio.

"Oh, that's quick. I didn't think it would come so soon." Ellie was delighted. She unwrapped it carefully, unaware of Robin's impatience. "I asked Ed if he could send me one of these. But I didn't expect it to be framed as well. Wonderful, isn't she?"

The life-size image of Cartimandua, one time queen of the Brigantes, stared out of the frame. Robin felt as if she were being examined and somehow fell short of the queen's expectations. Ellie's delight was palpable and Robin's earlier insecurity resurfaced. She watched her lover as she caressed the picture before setting it on the ledge near her easel, a position from which the queen could watch her paint.

"Didn't you want Vellocatus as well?" Robin felt a sudden connection with the queen's consort, the forgotten woman.

"Not really. She never says much."

Maybe she didn't get a chance to get a word in, thought Robin. The strong, silent type, used to being in the background. She looked at the painting, Ellie's current work in progress. It didn't look like anywhere around the farm, the landscape was flatter, more meadow-like. There was something odd about it, but she couldn't put her finger on what it was.

"Where is this, Ellie?"

"It's the place where Cartimandua wants her bones to be interred. Her final resting place."

Robin raised her eyebrows. "She 'told' you that?"

"Yes. And now she's here, she can tell me if it looks right." Ellie's brilliant smile was heartbreaking. Robin wanted to rip the canvas off the easel and tear it into little pieces before starting on the picture of the queen. Ellie sensed her mood.

"It's all right, Rob. I'm not mad." Ellie wrapped an arm around her waist and looked up at her. "But just so you know, she thinks you're cute."

It had taken all the self-control she could muster not to react. Ellie was happy, that was all that mattered. Robin had kissed her and left her to commune with the queen. Now, a day later, she was wondering who she could talk to. Jo seemed to think it was quite natural to have conversations with someone who had been dead for almost two thousand years. She mentioned it to her when she got home from the market, but Jo had been in another place herself.

Harry wasn't any help but he was company. Talking to a dog must be saner than talking to a picture. He followed her back into the yard and flopped down next to her while she got out her tools. It wouldn't hurt to give the bike a once over, and Jo's van hadn't sounded too healthy when it limped up the lane yesterday. But before starting on either of the jobs Robin thought she could give Den a call. There was something else she needed to ask.

†

Autumn colors, the last of the leaves clinging onto the trees, the brightness of the oranges and golds against the pale blue sky, didn't match her mood. The swirling flow of the muddy brown water of the river as it passed under the bridge was more in tune with how she was feeling.

Den leaned against the stone parapet and watched the people walking past. They all had purpose, making their way to homes, to shops, to restaurants.

In the few days since their return from London, Den had felt her initial joy at Kathryn's acceptance of her proposal seeping away. She had watched the professor twisting the ring on her finger, looking like she wanted to take it off, put it in a small plastic bag, label it, and file it away in a drawer for unusual finds.

Kathryn was at the university. Wednesday was a heavy lecture day for her. Den had found herself stuck on a tricky point in the article she was writing and came out for a walk to clear her head. Instead she found herself dissecting her relationship and thinking Henry had been right. Kathryn probably wasn't ready yet to take a big step like marriage.

Her phone pinged. She pulled it out. Message from Robin: *"Can u talk?"* She found Robin's number in her contacts and pressed it. Robin answered right away.

"What's up, bud?"

"I've been meaning to call you about a few things. First off, I had this weird meeting on Monday morning. A prospective client."

"What was weird about it?"

"Well, they clearly wanted a PR person. That's not what I do. I could have done a great website for them but they're a big company. They probably have a team of people on that. No, it was more like they wanted to check me out."

"Why?"

"I think it's something to do with Jas. And I remembered afterwards something you asked me a while back. In the summer."

"What was that? I've slept a few times since then."

"Yeah. Well, you asked if Jas liked it rough. You thought she might be getting into something heavy duty. You wouldn't happen to remember the name, would you?"

Den thought for a moment. She vaguely remembered coming home one evening and Steph telling her about seeing Jas at a leather club. Something she'd found hard to believe at the time. "Um. Yeah, it was Steph who told me. Max somebody or other."

"Max Fleetwood."

"Yeah, that's it. A really hot dom was how Steph described her."

"Shit."

"Is that a problem?"

"I'm not sure. How did Jas end up with Steph?"

"I don't know. I was all over the place at the time, literally. Came home one night and they were shagging in my bed. Although Henry said they had been circling around each other like love-struck teenagers for a week."

"So, how did this Fleetwood woman connect Jas with me."

"Pillow talk. She could have mentioned you. So, are you going to do some work for her?"

"No way. The whole thing creeped me out."

Den started walking back through the town towards the apartment. "So, I guess you found Ellie, then."

"Oh, yeah, sorry. I should have let you know. But that's the other thing. Monday was one fucking weird thing after another. She talks to her."

"Sorry, you've lost me, mate. Who talks to who?"

"Ellie talks to Cartimandua. She's doing this painting. Says it's the place where the queen wants to be buried."

"Now that is weird. I hope you don't mind, but I think I should tell Kathryn. I mean, after the exhibition's finished they probably just stick the bones in a drawer somewhere in the bowels of the museum."

"Fine. Talk to her. I need someone who can make sense of this. Ellie doesn't think she's going mad, but it is driving me nuts."

After ending the call, Den walked the rest of the way home deep in thought.

†

Ash cycled past the lane again. A twenty-mile ride had seemed like a good idea on this fine autumn afternoon and she found herself drawn to the hills above Huddersfield. It had nothing to do with the thought of seeing a certain brown-eyed woman with a warm smile who looked pretty good even at four-thirty in the morning when she was wearing a baggy sweatshirt and jeans that had been hastily thrown on. Jo's appearance at the market the day before hadn't been enhanced by the collection of mismatched garments she'd been wearing, but there was something about her that was keeping Ash awake at night.

The last time she had been this way on her bike was during the club's evening ride when she'd had to endure twenty minutes pumping up hill with Shona Gibson's lycra-encased butt in her eye-line. Normally that was a view she would have enjoyed, but she and Shona weren't on the best of terms these days. When Ash had responded to the call-out to investigate at Starling Hill, she'd been reminded of that ride, so finding an enticing looking woman at the farm had been a welcome distraction.

She turned up the lane, finally deciding that perhaps a follow-up visit was necessary. Although it was a day off, she was a responsible police officer, first and foremost. Halfway up the long track she wondered if Jo would be there. She was relieved to see the brightly painted camper van parked near the farmhouse when she arrived in the yard.

At first Ash thought no one was around but then a head popped up from behind the gleaming Harley, the newest vehicle in the yard. Green eyes gave her a suspicious once-over but the voice wasn't unfriendly when the woman spoke.

"Can I help you?"

Ash took her helmet off and ran her fingers through her short hair. "I was looking for Jo. Her van's here."

"Yeah. Points for observation." The bike owner studied her for a moment longer before adding, "She's in the pottery studio. Over there."

"Okay. Thanks." Ash wheeled her bicycle towards the low building across from the house aware of the curious gaze following her, wondering if she'd walked into a dyke commune. She had been on leave when the media circus turned up at Starling Hill the year before, and when she returned, all the other officers could say about the event was that the owner of the farm, Eleanor Winters, was a babe.

The first room in the stable block was an art studio, and looked different in the daylight. Ash glanced at the canvas sitting on the easel by the low windows. The artist definitely had talent. She didn't realize she was staring until a voice asked, "Who are you?"

She turned to find herself looking at the "babe." Not really her type but she could see the attraction for her male colleagues. "Um, yeah, hi. I'm Ash. I was looking for Jo."

"She's in the next room, but you might want to wait until she's finished throwing."

"Throwing?"

"Forming the clay into a shape."

Listening now, Ash could hear the whirring noise of the pottery wheel. "Oh, right. So you must be Eleanor."

"Yes, but my friends call me Ellie. Are you from Hebden Bridge?"

"No."

"How do you know Jo, then?"

"We met a few days ago." Ash wondered if Jo had told Ellie about her nighttime jitters. She didn't want to embarrass her if she hadn't wanted to admit that she'd been frightened enough during the night to call the police.

"Okay. Well, if you go through, just wait until she's stopped the wheel before you speak to her."

"Thanks."

She followed the sound into the next room and leant against the wall enjoying the scene in front of her. Jo's concentration, her clay-encased hands around the object being formed: Ash was entranced once more.

†

Robin finished with her bike and was starting to take a look at the van's engine when Jo emerged from the studio with the stranger.

"I'll just wash my hands. Would you like coffee or tea?" she heard Jo ask as the pair came closer. Harry woke up from his position near her feet and bounded over to his owner.

"Meet Harry." The dog gave the newcomer a welcoming lick.

They had reached the van now. "Ash, this is Robin. She and Ellie are married."

Robin wasn't quite sure why that was part of the introduction. She held up her oily hands. "Hi. I won't shake hands, but nice to meet you."

"Yes, you too."

"Do you want a brew, Rob? Ellie's joining us."

"Sure. I won't be long here."

She watched them go into the house and smiled. It seemed Jo had an admirer. She deserved a break in the relationship department. Her last girlfriend had been no great loss in Robin's opinion. This one looked like she had something about her.

It didn't take long for her to see that the van needed an oil top up. She had put her tools away and was wiping her hands on a rag, thinking about going in for the coffee Jo would be making when she heard another vehicle approaching. It looked like a large coach.

Ellie emerged from the studio at the same time as the coach arrived in the yard. Robin ran over to join her and they watched as the doors opened and a young man with a clipboard emerged. He was smartly dressed and looked around brightly.

"Excuse me. What are you doing?" Robin confronted the man.

"This is Starling Hill farm, isn't it?"

"Yes."

"Great." He called back into the coach. "Come on down, folks. This is the place."

"The place for what?" Robin stood directly in front of him. She was a good head taller.

"The next stop on our tour. We're doing *Happy Valley* and *Last Tango in Halifax* locations and we've just added Starling Hill to the itinerary. People want to see where Queen Cartimandua and her consort lived and died."

"There's not much to see. It's just a field."

"That field there?" He pointed with his clipboard.

"Yes."

"Right. This way, everyone." Sightseers of all shapes and sizes and ages were spilling out into the yard. The young man led the way and they all followed.

Robin went back to Ellie and put her arm around her shoulders. They looked on in dismay as the group trouped over to the field. To his credit, the guide didn't let them go in. He waved his arms around, talking the whole time, sounding quite knowledgeable about the dig that had taken place and the discoveries made.

"They can't do this, can they?" Ellie was shaking.

"I don't think we can stop this lot now they're here. But I'll find out who's running this tour and have words with them. They certainly shouldn't have shown up here unannounced. It's private land."

Ten minutes later the coachload was gone. Ellie watched the vehicle disappear down the lane and heaved a sigh of relief.

"Why do they want to come to look at a field? They were even taking pictures."

"I know, hon." Robin didn't tell her that there were several Facebook groups devoted to Starling Hill, and Twitter was littered with hashtags for Cartimandua and Vellocatus, and the most popular of these was *#lesboqueen.*

"Kathryn said this wouldn't happen."

"I doubt the professor could have guessed, she probably doesn't watch much telly. It's just unfortunate we're in the same area as the locations used for those TV shows." Robin couldn't believe she was defending Dr. Kathryn Moss, the woman she thought of as her rival for Ellie's affections. Living rival anyway. "She wouldn't know this area's become as popular for filming as Northern Ireland and Dubrovnik." She gave Ellie a squeeze. "Come on, let's go and meet Jo's new friend."

†

Jasmine felt her self-confidence draining away as she scanned the faces in the room. It had been easy to come to these kinds of events when she was part of a company, bolstered with the armor of Armadillo. Now, she felt exposed, naked. She wished she had taken Steph up on the offer to accompany her. Her lover's sturdy presence would have steadied her nerves.

All of PR London seemed to be here. Rumor had it that the mayor would be making an entrance, but there was no sign of the famous blond mop anywhere. She surveyed the groups of well-groomed people, all looking as if they were talking about important things, but in reality doing the same visual checks as everyone else.

Come on Jas, you've done this kind of thing a million times. You can schmooze it up with the best of them.

The black dress was a looser fit than the last time she had worn it, but she still felt it clinging to her curves, still warm from Steph's touch. She'd left the house with Steph's words ringing in her ears, "You are all mine, babe. No one else touches this."

Steph had slipped her hand into Jas's panties and deftly maneuvered two fingers inside the lips still swollen from their earlier lovemaking. Jas only just had time to change her underwear again before the taxi arrived, leaving Steph smirking at her from their bed.

Grabbing a glass of Champagne from a passing tray, Jasmine moved further into the room. She saw someone she knew from another agency and made her way over to their group. "Hey, Sarah. Long time no see." They exchanged air kisses on both cheeks.

"So, Jas, I gather you've struck out on your own. Joined the ranks of the unemployed, sorry I mean, freelancers." Sarah's smile was friendly but Jas could sense the mockery behind it.

She smiled back. "Yes. It's good. I should have done it a long time ago."

"This is Jason. He joined us last year." Sarah introduced her to the man she was with, an earnest-looking suit. "And Monica, our rising star and social media expert."

Monica's beauty queen looks didn't fit the geek stereotype, but then she wouldn't have pegged Robin for one either when she first met her. If she hadn't known Sarah was straight, she would have thought Monica had been hired purely for her looks.

Before either Monica or Jason had a chance to say anything, another voice broke into their grouping. "Well, well, what have we here? A rare sighting of a delicate little bird."

Jasmine froze. She knew that voice without having to turn her head. Sarah's group melted away as a strong arm landed across her shoulders. She looked up into the smooth, unsmiling face of Max Fleetwood.

"So naughty." Max released her and moved around to stand in front of her. "Just smile and sip your drink. Look like we're having a chat."

Cold eyes appraised her, moving up and down her body. "You've lost some weight, chicken. But, still enough padding to make our fun and games interesting."

"Max, I don't think…"

"No, you don't. No one runs from me." The frown had turned into a sneer.

Jas looked around, but there were only the backs of oblivious groups of strangers. She fought back the tears that were threatening.

"Hi Jas. Sorry, am I interrupting something?"

She looked at the newcomer and almost leapt into his arms in relief. "No, not at all. What are you doing here?"

Max moved away but not before saying, "Good to see you Jasmine. We'll catch up later."

"Are you okay, Jas? You look like you're going to faint. Who was she?" Paul was looking at her quizzically.

Jasmine let out a big breath of air. "You don't want to know, Paul. But thank you for your timely intervention. What *are* you doing here?"

"I came with Ted. He wanted some moral support. Henry's just back from a trip and didn't feel like partying."

Another man came over to them then holding two glasses. He handed one to Paul. She vaguely remembered having met him at the house during one of Henry's dinner parties. "Ted, you remember Jas. She lives in our house, with Steph."

"Oh, yes. You're with Armadillo, aren't you?"

"Not any more. I've gone freelance."

"Oh right. How's that going?"

"It's going. I'm still finding my feet." She looked at Paul. "I'm not feeling too good. I think I'll head home now."

"Don't you want to wait for the mayor? He should liven things up." Ted knocked back most of his Champagne in one gulp.

She only managed a wan smile. Paul handed his glass back to Ted. "Come on. I'll put you in a taxi."

He waited with her until the taxi arrived. She gave him a quick hug. "Thank you so much."

The tears she'd been holding back for what seemed like hours, flooded out as soon as she was inside the house. Steph emerged from the living room.

"Shit, babe. What's wrong?"

Jasmine felt her lover's arms envelop her. She sobbed freely on her shoulder. When she'd calmed down, Steph guided her into the living room and sat her down on the couch. She took her shoes off and knelt in front of her, gently massaging her feet.

"Tell me. If anyone's hurt you, I'll kill them."

"No! I don't want you going anywhere near her."

"Her!" Steph's eyes widened as understanding set in. "Max."

"Yes. If Paul hadn't turned up, I don't know what would have happened."

"Did she threaten you?"

Jas started crying again. Steph quickly joined her on the couch and held her close again. "It's okay, babe. I'm here." She stroked her hair. "We're not going to let that psycho bitch ruin things for us. Remember what I said earlier. You're mine. And I'll protect you with everything I've got."

†

Jo left Ash in the living room getting more closely acquainted with Soames while she went into the downstairs loo to wash her hands. Her reflection in the mirror showed a tangled mass of hair that needed a good comb through. If anything she looked worse than when Ash had seen her at the market.

She headed into the kitchen and set up the coffeemaker. It started to gurgle into life as she put a mismatched assortment of mugs out on the counter. The cupboard held two shelves worth of misshapen items—failed pottery creations, some of which were now hers. She was rather fond of the one that looked like a piece of molded driftwood.

Ash was sitting where she'd left her when she returned to the living room, leaving the coffeemaker to do its thing for the next five minutes. Not that Ash could have moved with Soames taking up residence on her lap. She looked up when Jo came in.

"Is that your guitar?" she asked, nodding towards the instrument, which was propped up by the bookcase.

"Yes."

"Play something for me?"

"I'm not that good. I just play around with it for myself really."

"Aw, come on. Please."

Jo smiled at her and fetched the guitar. Positioning it in front of her body, she perched on the edge of the armchair and plucked at the strings before settling on a song to play. A love song would be too obvious, so she started in on the good old standby, "Blowin' in the Wind." Robin came in just as she finished the last chorus with Ash joining in enthusiastically, but slightly out of tune.

"Shit! You're not a folkie as well, are you?" Robin called as she walked quickly past and up the stairs.

Ellie came in more slowly followed by Harry. Jo stood, relinquishing the armchair.

"You don't have to move," Ellie said.

"No, it's fine. The coffee should be ready now." She put the guitar back in its place and headed into the kitchen. She loaded up a tray with four mugs of coffee, milk, sugar, and spoons. When she returned to the living room, Harry had attached himself to Ash resting his head on her knee, trying to get her attention away from the ginger cat. Jo was relieved to set the tray down on the coffee table in front of the sofa without spilling anything.

Robin returned staring intently at her iPad. "Got it," she said, going over to Ellie. She showed her the screen. "See. Says it right here on their itinerary. 'Visit the recently discovered burial site of the legendary Queen Cartimandua in the heart of Brigantes territory.'"

"What's that?" Jo asked, sitting down next to Ash but leaving a respectable space between them.

"Bloody coach tour just turned up. First thing we knew of it. They can't just do that, can they? This is private land."

"Ash might know."

"Why? Are you a lawyer?"

Jo winced at Robin's abrupt tone, but Ash just answered calmly. "No. Police officer."

"Okay. So, what can we do to stop them. Legally."

"Well, I'm not an expert on this kind of thing. But, first off, this tour company should have asked your permission. If you don't want them here, you will have to let them know. To restrict access generally you'll have to install a gate at the end of your lane and put on a 'No Trespassing' notice. That won't stop people climbing over it. But it's quite a hike from there and might discourage them."

"Won't discourage the fucking ramblers. We get them all the time, claiming they have the 'right to roam'."

"Calm down, sweetie." Ellie placed a hand on Robin's arm. "We can talk about this later. So, Ash, you're a keen cyclist?"

"Yes. I belong to a cycling club. But on days like this when I'm not working, it's great to get out for a ride."

"Have you come far today?"

"Not really. About ten miles to here, twenty round trip."

Robin had finally sat down next to Jo. "That's far enough on these roads. How long does that take?"

"An hour, more or less."

After their coffee, leaving Robin still glaring at her iPad, Jo suggested they go outside. Harry joined them as they walked across the yard to the field.

"Is this what all the fuss is about?"

"Well, it was exciting when the dig was on. It was Harry who discovered the first bone, you know. If it wasn't for him, the skeletons might not have been discovered. I mean, Dr. Moss only thought there might have been a

Roman fort of some kind here. She wasn't expecting to find any bones. And they turned out to be not just any old bones."

Ash leaned against the gate and looked across the smooth turf. "It looks very peaceful now."

"Yeah. I guess you can understand why Ellie's not keen on coach parties turning up."

They stood watching Harry as he raced around. He stopped at a particular spot and pawed the ground.

"He always goes back there. Even with the new turf, he knows."

"That's where he found the first bone?"

"Yes. He was very upset when I had to drag him away, leaving it behind. He hasn't forgotten." Jo called to him. He looked over and reluctantly made his way back up towards them, making a show of stopping to pee on blades of grass.

"Um, Jo?"

"Yes." Jo found herself gazing into intense blue eyes.

"Would you have dinner with me?"

"When?"

"Tonight. Short notice, I know, but I'm back on the evening shift tomorrow. Three 'til eleven."

"I don't think we'll get far on your bike."

"I have a car." Ash gave her a tentative smile. "Pick you up at seven?"

"Okay. This car, it doesn't have blue and yellow stripes and flashing lights, does it?"

"Not unless you want it to."

"Seven o'clock then."

"Great." Ash's smile broadened.

Jo watched her cycle down the lane and spoke to the dog now standing by her side. "How about that, Harry? Looks like I've got a date. Now, what am I going to wear?"

Back in the house, Jo found Robin and Ellie in the kitchen. Robin was washing up the coffee mugs while Ellie gathered together ingredients for their evening meal.

"I'm going out for dinner," she announced.

Robin turned from the sink and grinned at her. "Looks like you've hooked one there, Jo."

"Yes, she seems nice." Ellie looked up from her inspection of the potatoes she'd selected. "How did you meet her?"

"She arrested you for singing in a public place."

"Robin!"

"Um, well, it's a bit embarrassing actually." Jo told them how she'd been frightened while they were away and called the police. "Ash turned up on her own and had a look around for me. I had to apologize for bringing her all the way out here for nothing. She said it made a nice change from breaking up doggers."

Robin laughed and Ellie looked at her, puzzled. "Doggers?"

"Oh, Ellie. You have led a sheltered life. There's probably a lot of it going on around here. You explain it to her, Robin. I need to see if I've got anything to wear tonight."

Jo could hear their laughter as she reached the bottom of the stairs. She knew that the couple indulged in outdoor sex themselves, but at least it was private, on their own land. She couldn't understand the appeal of "dogging" herself, of meeting up in parking areas to watch other people having sex and getting off on it.

†

Threading her way through the throngs of students and tourists filling the narrow street leading to the Market Place, Kathryn's mind ranged back to the discussions with Ed McLaughlin about the DNA project. He thought it was worth a shot even though he was finding it hard to garner support from other colleagues.

"We know which general matrilineal haplogroup Cazza was in. Could probably have worked that out without DNA tests as most Northern Europeans share it. But to work out the Y chromosome mutations we have nothing concrete to go on. And as Cazza became queen, there were obviously no male heirs to take over leadership of the tribe. The male line must have died with her father."

"But there is evidence to suggest that her ex-husband, Venutius, was related to her. A cousin."

"Still too generalized. Anyone who's interested will already have paid for a haplogroup DNA test. Why pay extra just to find out if you might be distantly related to Queen Cartimandua?"

"You may be right, Ed. I'll think about it."

Kathryn's thoughts were still on the questions posed by Ed as she reached the door to the flat. Letting herself in she was aware of the lack of cooking smells. She didn't think they had plans to go out that evening. Den's cooking skills were fairly limited, but she had learned how to do a decent pasta dish over the last few months. Kathryn left her coat and briefcase in the hall. Definitely no activity in the kitchen. She poured herself a glass of white wine from the bottle in the fridge.

"Den!"

No answer. She put her glass down and walked through to Den's office. The journalist was stuffing something into her rucksack, the large one she'd brought with her when she moved in.

"Den? Going somewhere?"

"Yeah. Got a job in London." Den looked at her then and Kathryn was shocked by the sadness in her eyes.

"For God's sake, Den. What's wrong?"

"I don't know. You tell me."

Kathryn reached out to her. "I don't understand."

"No, you don't. That's the problem." Den grasped her hand, the one with the ring on it. "I don't think you want this, do you? I'm sorry. I rushed you."

The front door intercom buzzed.

Den let go of her hand. "That'll be the taxi."

Kathryn was stunned. "I…can't we sit down and talk about this."

"When I get back. I have to go now."

"How long will you be gone?"

"I don't know." She picked up the rucksack and brushed past her.

Kathryn followed her down the hallway. "Call me when you get there. Okay?"

"Okay."

Den was gone without a backward glance. Kathryn watched the taxi drive away. She walked back into the flat and leant against the door, sliding slowly to the floor. What was this all about? Den was right. She really didn't understand. They hadn't had a fight about anything that she could recall. Maybe she'd been a bit preoccupied lately but the exhibition and the new term at the university, a new job, it all required her full attention. She thought Den knew that and was adapting to life in Durham. But maybe the trip to London had made her realize what she was missing. Or maybe it was the same old thing, her own sadly lacking finesse in relationship skills.

Kathryn twisted the ring on her finger as the emptiness of the apartment settled around her and the tears started to fall.

†

Ash checked her image in the mirror. Her hair was growing back slowly but she was happy with the length it was now. And she'd stopped having to pencil in her eyebrows now that they had grown as well. Rescuing the elderly man from the burning car had been worth the effort though. The man had survived and his family was grateful. Her boss had been less enthusiastic about her heroics. "What if he'd been some scum drug dealer? You wouldn't be so keen to risk your own life for him, would you? I can't afford to lose good officers, Ashworth. Think before you do anything so stupid again."

"Yes sir," had been the only response she could give without sounding insubordinate. But she had caught the smile in his eyes as she turned to leave his office.

The choice of clothing for the evening hadn't been difficult. Her non-uniform wardrobe consisted of either cycling gear or jeans and t-shirts. She did, however, have several tailored shirts that didn't look too much like the ones she wore for work. She chose the brightest one, magenta with a light pink stripe running through it. Blue would suit her eyes better, but she was heartily sick of the color blue by the end of her shifts.

As she drove up to the farm, this time in her nearly new Audi A3, Ash wondered what it was about Jo Bright Flame that had her prepared not only to cycle twenty miles that day, but also to make the round trip again for a dinner date. She hadn't dated anyone since her fall out with Shona Gibson. Bad timing she figured, for both of them. The woman had been on the rebound from her last relationship and was carrying more baggage than a transatlantic airbus. Ash wasn't going to unburden her own weighty load to someone who would likely only be passing in transit. That encounter made her realize she still wasn't ready for a romantic relationship of any kind, and there were days when she wondered if she ever would be again.

Jo's lifestyle was the complete opposite to her well-ordered life. Ash had known from an early age that she wanted to be a police officer. She loved the job. She had started as a volunteer cadet from the age of thirteen, and now was coming up to her thirty-years' service. Then it would be time to decide what to do next.

Ash met plenty of people like Jo through the job but not one she would have wanted to spend more time with than necessary. She'd had her fill of well-meaning protesters caught up in the madness of a peaceful demonstration hijacked by the loonier left. The front line of a riot squad wasn't her idea of a fun-filled night out. Ash could see Jo as a fully paid up member of the placard waving, marching community, hair flying out behind her, linking arms with her comrades to face the police barricade.

So, why was she attracted to her? This was the question she had wrestled with on her ride home, and now on the journey back in the car. She turned up the track leading to the farm wondering if she wasn't just having some kind of mid-life pre-menopausal crisis.

Whatever doubts Ash had been entertaining disappeared when Jo came out of the house. Her hair, now tangle free, had the glow of being freshly washed. And her wide smile when Ash greeted her and opened the passenger door made the evening come alive.

†

Once they were settled at their corner table near the fireplace, Ash asked the question that had been on her mind.

"You said you were living on a barge boat on the canal. What made you move to the farm? It's a bit of a trek to Hebden for the market." For an awkward few moments she didn't think Jo would answer.

Finally Jo looked up at her and gave her a small smile. "I didn't see it coming although the signs were there." She paused and Ash waited. Interview technique number one—wait for the suspect to talk—silence always unnerves the more nervous ones.

"It was Molly's boat," Jo continued. "We met one night at a concert and it seemed like we had a lot in common. She invited me to come and look at her crafts. She was gearing up for the summer months and had managed to snag a prime position near the town center for the barge. Anyway, one thing led to another and then we were living together."

"Sounds ideal."

"It was, for a time. Then it was like a tap turning off. One day she was all lovey-dovey, the next I was getting the cold shoulder. Turns out she had it all planned. The mooring lease had run out and she was moving the barge back down to Stoke, which was where she'd come from. I wasn't part of the plan."

"Wow, that sucks."

"Yeah. Luckily I had kept the camper van. Wade and Ian stored it for me in their garage. Sort of a thank you for when I looked after their house while they were in Canada. I saw Robin one day when she'd finished her boxing class and was wandering through the market. When I told her what had happened she offered a place straight away, telling me there was no way I should even think of wintering in the van."

Before Ash could comment on this, the waiter turned up to ask what they would like to drink. Ash ordered a coke and Jo asked for a glass of red wine.

"I know it's because you're driving this evening, but don't you drink at all?"

"Sometimes, the occasional beer or glass of wine. But I can't afford to lose my license and my job."

"Do you like driving?"

"Yes. I'm mostly on traffic."

"I thought that was an unpopular job." Jo looked genuinely puzzled. "On cop shows, detectives are always being threatened with being demoted to traffic, writing out parking tickets."

"Hell, no. It's the best job, really. I love it. Arresting nob-heads who drink and drive or talk on their phones. Getting dangerous idiots off the road seems like a worthwhile occupation to me. And it's more fun than dealing with domestics. Hate those call-outs where you end up wading through shit in people's so-called living rooms."

"Dog shit?" Jo was staring at her, wide-eyed.

"No, human. The way some folks live, it's worse than anything you've seen on TV."

Their drinks arrived and the conversation stalled as they studied the menu. During the meal they talked about their childhoods and Ash was surprised to find that it was something they had in common. Jo's father had been in the army, where Ash's had been in the air force. Both of them had moved around from base to base in the UK and Europe. Ash had fond memories of the time their family had spent at the NATO RAF base on the Dutch and German border. Jo's family had been based in Germany for a few years, but it was while she was in primary school, and she hadn't retained much of the language she had picked up then.

It was while they were on their coffee that Ash remembered the picture and the observation she had made at the time. "Have you noticed, Jo? That framed photo in Ellie's studio. There's an uncanny resemblance between Ellie and the woman in it."

"That's Cartimandua. And it's only an artist's impression."

"Yes, but you have a look. It's in the eyes."

"The reconstruction team only had a two thousand year old skull to work from. It's amazing that the color of her eyes and hair can be discovered through DNA testing, even after so long. Ellie certainly does seem to have a connection with the queen. I've heard her talking while she's painting. Robin mentioned it to me yesterday. I think she's worried about Ellie's sanity."

"They seem pretty solid as a couple."

"Well, they went through a rough patch during the dig. And Robin's not been known for her fidelity, but she seems more settled now."

"You and Robin…?" Ash had sensed something earlier at the farm.

"It was a one off. But, yes, that's how I got to know them. Ellie took me on as a pottery student."

"What? Even though she knew you and Robin had…"

"Yes. But she didn't see me as a threat. She had Jasmine to worry about at the time."

"And Jasmine is…?"

"She lives in London but she thought Robin was in love with her. It was weird. I mean, we all turned up at the farm on the same day…me, Jasmine, and Dr. Moss. She and Ellie had something going for a while."

"Jesus! Is there something in the air up there? Sounds like there's more going on than in your average soap opera."

"Yeah. But now it's fine. Robin and Ellie got married. Dr. Moss is with Den, the journalist, and from what Robin said when they got back, they're now engaged. And Jasmine's with someone else as well. So, happy endings all round."

"Except for you."

"I've got Harry."

Lucky Harry, was Ash's thought as she was captured once more by Jo's smile and clear brown-eyed gaze. She was sure she could offer her more than the dog. On the way back to the farm she knew she wanted to see her again and there were things she should talk to her about but it wasn't something she wanted to do in a public place.

†

It looked like a toss-up between reruns of *Midsomer Murders* or *Downton Abbey*. With Paul out for the evening, Henry was at a loose end. He'd given up trying to read the book his co-pilot had recommended—a best seller she'd picked up at their last layover in Singapore and passed on to him. But he found he couldn't care less what happened to any of the characters. So, *Downton* it was. He could always fantasize about the possibility of backstairs hanky-panky between Thomas and the hunky new footman.

The front door banged shut, startling him from the doze he'd fallen into only ten minutes after the program's start. Den came into the room and dumped her heavy rucksack on the floor.

"Hey, hotshot reporter, what are you doing here?" He muted the sound on the TV.

She collapsed onto the sofa next to him. "Just waiting for you to say 'I told you so'."

"Told you what?"

"That it was too soon to ask her to marry me. It's not what she wants, Hen."

To his dismay, she burst into tears.

"Oh shit. Come here." He hugged her and waited for the tears to subside. They'd known each other since they were kids and he hated seeing her like this, full of emotional turmoil. But then he'd never seen her in love before.

He got up and fetched the box of tissues from the bookcase. "Here. I'll go get us a drink. I definitely need one now."

When he returned with two glasses of malt whisky, she had dried her tears and was looking at her phone.

"She's sent me a text. But I can't talk to her right now."

"Okay. But, I don't get it. You two looked great at the exhibition. You looked happy. That's only a few days ago. What's happened?"

"Nothing."

Henry waited and sipped his drink. He glanced at the screen. Thomas was standing in the scullery with an 'If I don't get a fuck soon, I'm out of here' look on his face. But most of the cast probably felt that way, even the Dowager Countess.

Den gulped back a large mouthful of whisky. Henry watched the color come back into her face.

"So, nothing's brought you on a three-hour train journey."

"I don't know, Hen. I just need some time on my own. And I think she does too."

"So, why can't you talk to her?"

"I just can't. I can't bear it when she shuts me out."

"How does she do that?"

"She just does. She doesn't even know she's doing it."

"Okay. But it doesn't mean she doesn't love you. In her own way. I mean, I thought that was part of her appeal for you."

They sat together in silence. Henry turned the television off; he knew what was going to happen there anyway. The phone rang, breaking into their individual thoughts. Henry hesitated before getting up to answer it. The only calls they got now on their landline were usually sales calls but it was too late even for the most persistent of cold callers.

"Hello."

"Henry. Is Den there?" Kathryn's voice sounded far away.

"Yes, she's here." He turned to Den, holding the receiver out to towards her. "It's Kathryn." Den looked up and shook her head. He grimaced at her before speaking into the phone again. "I'm sorry, Kathryn. It seems she's indisposed right now."

"Is she all right?"

"Yes, I think so. Look, it's late. We all need some sleep. She might feel like talking to you tomorrow."

"Okay." He could hear the break in her voice as she spoke the next words so quietly he almost didn't catch them. "Tell her I love her, please."

"Yes. I'll tell her that. Thanks for calling. Goodnight." He put the phone down carefully.

Den was staring at the floor between her feet, head in her hands.

"She asked me to tell you she loves you."

"Yeah. Sure she does."

"For God's sake, Den. This is more depressing than an episode of *Eastenders*. Can't you two get your shit together without behaving like a couple of kids with more hormones than brains?"

Den looked up at him then with the flicker of a smile. "That about sums it up, doesn't it? I think you're right about sleep though. Is my bed still free?"

"I haven't rented it out to any passing dykes, if that's what you mean." He was referring to the time she'd arrived home in the summer and found Jas and Steph making out in her bed.

She laughed out loud and gave him a proper smile for the first time since her arrival. "Okay. Thanks, Hen. See you in the morning. Maybe I'll be able to think straight then." She stood and pecked him on the cheek before picking up her rucksack and heading up the stairs.

He watched her go thinking, *I somehow doubt it*. Checking his watch he realized he only had five hours before Paul got home expecting a cooked breakfast. Turning out the lights he made his way up the stairs and went into his bedroom.

Part Two

Questions

Chapter Four

The last person Jas expected to see when she came down for breakfast on Thursday morning was Den. The journalist was sitting in the kitchen, drinking coffee and reading the newspaper.

"Hi. When did you get here?"

Den looked up and Jas could see the tiredness in her eyes. "Last night. Bit late."

"Oh, right. Staying long?"

"I don't know."

She didn't have to spell it out. More Kathryn trouble. Jas really didn't know why her friend was hooked on the professor. The woman's so-called charm had never worked for her. She poured herself a coffee. With the quality beans Henry insisted on, Jas found she actually enjoyed drinking it without any enhancements. Desire for full fat lattes was a thing of the past.

"Well, I'm glad you're here." Jas placed a slice of whole meal bread in the toaster.

'Oh?"

"Yeah. Something I need to talk to you about. Do you want any toast?" she asked, getting out the butter and marmalade.

"No, thanks."

Jas brought her coffee and toast over to the table and sat down opposite Den. She buttered the toast slowly and looked up to find Den staring at her.

"Well, what's up?"

"You remember that woman I was seeing? Before Steph."

"The one you wouldn't tell me about."

Jas sipped her coffee, inhaling the rich aroma. "Her name is Max Fleetwood. I did really like her and the sex was hot."

Den held up her hand. "TMI, Jas. Stop there."

"No, really. But it got a bit out of hand. And to cut a long story short, Steph rescued me."

"I wondered how you two got together."

"Anyway, that's the main reason I left my job. I didn't want to risk seeing her again. But then, I went to this PR event on Tuesday and…" Jas felt the tears welling up again.

"And she was there." Den finished the sentence for her, reaching across the table to hold her hand.

Jas nodded, embarrassed by her tears.

"Look, this is a bit weird. Robin called me. She had a meeting with this Max on Monday." Den kept hold of her friend's hand.

"What!"

"She thought it was odd because obviously the job wasn't something she would do. She got the idea Max was checking her out."

"Oh, shit! I thought she would have moved on to someone else by now. I don't want any of you to get caught up in this. How would she know about Robin?"

"Good question."

Jas wiped away her tears and looked across at her friend. "I just...I'm so happy with Steph. I don't want anything to spoil it."

"From what I've seen, she cares for you as well. I wouldn't worry about this Max person. It'll sort itself out."

"You don't know her. She's very powerful, in business as well as in her private life."

"Everyone has their weak spots. And the higher up they are, the further they have to fall." Den gave her a reassuring smile. "Trust me, I'm a journalist."

Jas laughed. "I've heard that before. So, anyway, what are your plans for the day?"

"I've got some people to see. Heading into town in a while. You?"

"I'm working up a PR schedule for a new client. Then I'll be going into town as well. Do you want to meet up?"

"Sure. Let me guess. Starbucks?"

"Nope. I've gone cold turkey on their coffees. I was thinking more along the lines of a Champagne Cocktail somewhere."

"I like your thinking. But there's probably not much difference in the calorie count."

"No, but it's more fun."

They agreed on a time and place and Jas headed back up the stairs to what had once been Den's room in the house and was now hers and Steph's. The gardener had left early as she usually did on weekdays and, as Jas settled down in front of her laptop, she let her mind wander back to their morning lovemaking, easing her worries about Max Fleetwood.

†

Lunch with Jas had been fun. By an unspoken agreement they avoided discussion of Kathryn and the reason why Den was in London. Den's meeting with her former boss at the paper had been unproductive. He didn't have any freelance work for her. The features editor at the archaeology magazine was more positive. He'd been impressed with her article about the Durotriges tribes from her Dorset trip in the summer. He gave her the names of some sources to tap for a follow-up article.

When she parted from Jas, they were both feeling the buzz from the bottle of Champagne they'd shared while sucking back oysters. After the first glass of fizz, Den had worked up the courage to ask Jasmine about her weight loss and she confessed to becoming a gym bunny under Steph's influence.

Jas had gone on to an afternoon meeting with a potential client and Den decided to walk off some of the effects of the drink with a stroll by the Thames.

The trees had been in full leaf last time she'd walked along here. Now the branches were mostly bare with the onset of winter, although the temperature was milder than she was getting used to up north.

Her phone pinged. She looked at the screen—Robin.

"Hi."

"Hi, thought I should check up on you."

"Why?"

"Your Facebook status changed from 'Engaged' to 'It's Complicated' overnight. So what's up? That's got to be the shortest engagement on record."

"Yeah, well, it's complicated."

"I'm an expert on complicated, so…give."

"I think I sort of rushed her into it. It's what I want, but she's not really ready for it."

"Where are you?"

"London."

"Oh."

Robin managed to put a lot of meaning into that one syllable.

"I just needed some space. She's rung a few times but I don't feel I can talk to her right now."

"But you should talk to her. Shouldn't you?"

"I guess. I'm just not ready yet."

"Well, you can't just fester away down there. Why don't you come up here for a few days?"

"I don't want to impose on you."

"That's what we're here for, your bail out chums. Shit happens, you come to us."

Den smiled. Robin could always cheer her up. "All right. I'll think about it."

"Don't think too hard. We'll expect you sometime tomorrow."

With those words she was gone. Den leant against the wall and looked down onto the muddy edge of the riverbank. The tide was out, exposing the debris of careless humans, cans, plastic bottles, and unidentifiable objects. An archaeologist's treasure trove of the future. Ancient civilizations, supposedly less technologically adept, left behind exquisitely crafted jewelry and weaponry. The artefacts of the present would surely depict a proper dark age.

Thinking about archaeology wasn't a good idea. Den could feel her chest tightening again as she thought of the little hope she had for her own future, given the mistakes of her most recent past.

†

Another misshapen lump formed under her hands. Jo stopped the wheel. It was no good; her concentration was shot. Ever since the dinner date with Ash, she hadn't been able to focus on making anything with her creative muse on vacation. Harry had benefitted by being taken for long walks.

At least Kieran wasn't there to chastise her for wasting clay. The potter who shared the use of Ellie's kiln was in Australia. He planned to be there until February, visiting his son and baby grandson, and missing out on most of the winter months. But Jo could have used his presence now. Ellie was immersed in her painting and Jo didn't feel she could ask for her help.

Looking into Ash's blue eyes as they stood outside the farmhouse door the other night, Jo had been sure she was going to kiss her. But then she'd backed off with a hasty goodnight and got back into her car. Before they'd left the restaurant, Ash had said she would call her when she could. But so far there had been no call.

Jo went over the conversation during dinner and wondered if she might have said something to put her off, but nothing came to mind. So, maybe nothing was going to come of this, although she would have liked it to. And she was sure the attraction was there from Ash. But the differences in their lifestyles was probably too much of a leap for the police officer to take. Why would she want to hook up with a homeless drifter? Jo really did need to get her act together. At this rate she would soon be walking the streets with a shopping trolley full of her worldly goods, with poor Harry trailing along on a string behind.

†

The wet gray day suited Kathryn's mood. It was two days since Den had left and she still hadn't phoned. She ignored her messages and when Kathryn phoned the house again, Henry said she was out. And he'd assured her that really was the case; he wasn't just saying it to stop her speaking to Den.

Kathryn had been functioning on automatic pilot for the walk home and was startled by the mewling sound at her feet as she put the numbers into the entry keypad. A bedraggled bundle of fur with sad eyes was staring up from under the bush by the door.

The rain was beating down mercilessly and, relieved to get inside, she propped her umbrella, still partially open, against the wall and set her briefcase next to it. The small creature's cries reached her through the closed door. Coat half off, she shrugged it back on and opened the door. Bending down she could see that it was a kitten, and when she stretched her hand out it didn't move away. A tiny pink tongue flicked out.

"What are you doing here?" She picked it up. The frail frame was shaking. "Well, you better come in, then."

Kathryn carried it into the kitchen and set it down on the floor, removing her wet coat and draping it over a chair.

"We might have some milk, although I'm not sure cats are really supposed to drink milk." The small carton in the fridge was still half full. Finding a shallow bowl to pour the liquid into, she set it down on the floor. The kitten was looking around, wide-eyed. She nudged the bowl nearer and after a brief tentative sniff, the small creature started to lap enthusiastically.

If Den had been there she was sure a remark about 'wet pussies' would have been uttered by now. Looking around for something to dry it off, she decided to use a few sheets of kitchen roll. She gave the kitten a rub down when it had finished drinking, and then picked it up, cradling it with one arm while pouring herself a glass of red wine.

"Let's go and sit in a comfy chair."

The kitten fell asleep on her lap almost immediately once they were settled. A faint purring noise came from it. Kathryn sipped her wine and watched the rain lashing against the window. The storm didn't look like letting up any time soon. She stroked the kitten's drying fur and the contented purr rose in volume. The coloring was mostly gray with some white on her chest and paws.

"I guess you can stay the night. But I'll have to take you to the RSPCA tomorrow. Someone might be missing you."

Not as much as I'm missing a certain someone. The phone call from Robin Fanshawe had caught Kathryn off guard. The woman was hardly a fan, but she had tracked her down and got through the department secretary's defense system. At first Kathryn wasn't sure what Robin was talking about. Yes, of course, she knew about Ellie's painting. But then it became clear she wasn't talking about the powerful image Ellie had created of Queen Cartimandua and her lover at Starling Hill—the painting now displayed at the British Museum's exhibition.

Kathryn sat back, her wine glass empty, but unable to move without disturbing the kitten. Robin had eventually made her understand this was a new painting; one Ellie was doing from memory. Only Ellie claimed it wasn't her memory, it was the queen's. She said the painting was where the queen wanted to be interred. That was the word she used, not buried, interred. The queen wanted a proper ceremony.

The professor hadn't given any thought to what would happen to the bones once the exhibition was over. The museum would want the space for a new exhibit. Was it worth a trip to Starling Hill to see what Ellie was doing? The real question, she knew, was did she want to see Ellie again? The ring caught the light from the lamp when she moved her hand and blue sapphires winked at her.

She sighed, moved the kitten gently off her lap and onto the chair. Time to make another phone call.

†

Ellie felt Robin's arm snaking across her shoulders. She carried on chopping carrots without pause.

"What's up?" Ellie could always tell when her lover wanted something.

"I was thinking…"

"I've told you before, that's dangerous."

"I know. But what do you think about inviting Henry and Paul to come up this weekend?"

"It's a bit short notice. They probably already have plans if they're not working."

"Well, they can only say no."

"Okay, but…"

Robin had removed her arm and was already pressing the contact number on her phone. Ellie only heard her side of the conversation but it didn't take long. When the call ended, Robin grinned at her and punched the air.

"Yes, no problem. They're delighted. Should be here by lunchtime tomorrow."

"And where are they going to sleep?"

"I'll call the B&B in the village."

"They can't stay there."

"Why not? It's clean and they do a good breakfast."

"Not as good as mine." Ellie glared at her.

"Okay. Well, I'll talk to Jo. She won't mind moving into the study for a few nights. Then they can have the bed in Aiden's room."

Ellie smiled at the mention of her son's name. He had never lived permanently at the farm but the guest bedroom was always referred to as Aiden's.

"You'll change the sheets." It wasn't a question.

"Yes, of course." Robin grinned at her.

"What's going on here?"

"Nothing."

"Nothing is what you'll be getting to eat if you don't tell me." Ellie waved the chopping knife.

Robin shuffled her feet, looking about twelve. "Um, well, it's like this. Den's in London. She's had a falling-out with Kathryn and I think she'll probably come up with the boys. We can talk things over."

Ellie put the knife down and folded her arms across her chest. "And where's Den going to sleep, if she does come with them?"

"The sofa, I guess. I'll go into town in the morning and get whatever supplies we need."

"You really have been thinking." Ellie smiled. "I've had a thought as well."

"What's that?"

"I think you should come over here and kiss me." The new weekend plans meant there would be a house filled with people and she needed this intimate time with her lover. She relaxed into Robin's embrace and met her lips with a welcoming sigh. Dinner might have gone unmade if the sounds of Jo's guitar hadn't reached her ears before Robin's hands found their way under her shirt.

†

Paul checked the map. "I think we've missed it again, Hen. You should have been in that lane."

"Wake up grumpy drawers back there. She should know."

"I heard that."

"Well, help us out here? Do I have to go around again?" Henry was watching Den in the rearview mirror as she sat up and looked out the side window.

"We're passing the university."

"Yes, I can see that."

"Okay, no need to get your knickers in a twist. Take the second exit on this roundabout coming up."

"That's not the turn off on the instructions." Paul held up the Google Maps printout.

"No. But there is another way. It takes a bit longer, but it's more scenic."

"We're in your hands. Don't screw it up."

Den was surprised she remembered this route at all having only used it once. She had made the same mistake as Henry and took the chance rather than face another journey around the ring road. Den was relieved when she recognized landmarks and knew she was guiding Henry the right way. Once they passed the final cluster of houses, the countryside opened out onto the vast stretch of moorland while the road itself narrowed. She warned Henry to take it slowly as passing places were few and far between.

"God, I don't know how you managed this without getting a scratch on PJ."

PJ was the nickname for Henry's car, a white BMW, which she had borrowed for one of her trips in the summer. The journey in pursuit of Kathryn had taken her from

London to Durham to Blackpool to Starling Hill and back to London.

"Pride and Joy was never in any danger while I was driving," Den remarked blandly as Henry flinched every time they passed an encroaching stone wall. "You could go a bit faster. I'm dying for a pee."

"If you're that desperate, I'll pull into the next lay-by. You should have gone when we stopped at the last service station."

"Yes, dad."

"Oh, wow!" Paul craned his neck, looking around in wonder. "You can see for miles up here."

"Yeah. We're almost there. Don't blink, or you'll miss the turning." Den sat back and tried to quell the feeling of panic as they passed the opening to the field where she'd been shot at by the farmer after spending a long and terrifying night out on the moor. She closed her eyes. Robin's words from the day before came back to her. They certainly were her "bail out chums." The timely appearance of Robin and Ellie on that occasion had undoubtedly saved her life.

"Is this it?"

Henry's question brought her out of her reverie. "Yes. Take it slow. There are a few big potholes."

"Christ! If I'd known it was this bad I would have borrowed Steph's van."

Paul exclaimed again when they reached the farmyard. "Is that for real? Awesome!"

Den wondered what he was excited about then realized he was pointing at Jo's brightly painted VW camper van.

"Oh, yeah. I guess Jo's still here."

"Who is Jo?"

"She's a friend. She does pottery and makes other craft type things. If you sit still too long she'll probably read your palm."

"Oh, right. She's the hippie you told us about." Henry parked his car next to the van. "This is amazing, Den. It's just how you described it. I feel like I've been here before."

Den was already out of the car, stretching her long legs and inhaling a deep breath of country air. "Well, in a sense you have. There were massive photos on display in the museum." She reached back into the car for her jacket. The sun was deceiving as a cold wind made its presence known.

A black and white bundle of fur hurtled up to them and stopped, panting, in front of Paul who was examining the paintwork on the van closely. As he bent down, the dog moved in and licked his face.

"Harry!"

Den looked on with amusement as Jo approached. She wore an item of rainbow-patterned knitwear that she had no doubt made herself. The sweater was several sizes too big, hanging down past her thighs over red leggings, and disappearing into a well-worn pair of Ugg boots.

"So sorry. You haven't even been introduced yet." Jo pulled Harry away and made him sit.

Paul laughed. "Happens to me all the time. Being kissed by strange males."

"You wish." Henry put out his hand. "I'm Henry, the house-trained one. That's Paul."

Jo gave them both her wide smile and opened her arms. "Welcome to Starling Hill. I won't shake hands; mine need a wash. Your timing is brilliant. Robin just texted me to say lunch is ready."

"Oh, aren't we eating here?"

"Yes, but I was in the studio glazing some pots."

Den moved quickly towards the house. "Catch up with you in a minute, Jo." She heard Henry laughing as he told Jo why she was in a hurry. The coffee at the last motorway services stop had gone right through her and she really did need to find a toilet.

Robin met Den at the door. "Hey, glad you could make it."

"Yeah. The guys are really excited to be here." She was surprised when Robin pulled her into a hug. Shifting uncomfortably from foot to foot, she said as calmly as she could, "Um, Rob, you need to let go, unless you want me to pee on your feet."

"Right." Robin stepped back smartly. "Off you go. I'll let Ellie know you're all here."

Thankful for the release when she reached the loo and was able to finally empty her bladder, Den stared at herself in the mirror while she washed her hands. She figured she really did look like shit if Robin felt she needed a hug. There were bags under her eyes from lack of sleep. She hoped the fresh air and time spent with friends would dispel the turmoil she was feeling.

†

Henry had never been in this part of Yorkshire before. He had driven through the Dales but most of his walking holidays had been in the Lakes or the Peak District. A trip to Saddleworth Moor wouldn't have occurred to him as a holiday destination, but he was finding the scenery exhilarating with its mix of deep mysterious valleys and open barren moorland. The colors on the hillsides changed with the movements of the clouds. As a pilot, he spent a lot of time flying through and above cloud formations.

Paul had taken up Robin's offer of a bike ride and the roar of the engine disturbing the stillness indicated they were returning up the long track to the farm.

Ellie joined Henry by the gate to the field.

"I've seen quite a few sparrows and a number of thrushes, but no starlings," he said, turning to look at her.

"I don't know how the farm got its name. My father thought it was most likely named after previous owners called Starling rather than the bird. But that would be going back centuries."

"Your family has been here that long?"

"Dad did a lot of work on our family tree but couldn't get past the Civil War. He thought the original Winters were

Cromwell supporters and were given this land as a reward."
She smiled at him. "Although, considering where it is, maybe
it was a punishment."

The bike arrived at the top of the lane and Robin
brought it to a noisy stop in front of the farmhouse. Paul ran
over to them still wearing his helmet. "God, that was ace!
Don't you want a go, Hen?"

"No thanks. I prefer four wheels."

Robin arrived and removed Paul's helmet for him.
Henry noticed that she was a good head taller than his lover.

"So, what's the plan for tomorrow?" Paul asked.

"We thought we'd take a trip into Hebden Bridge,"
Ellie said. "Plenty of pubs and cafes to choose from for a spot
of lunch."

"Oh good. Can we visit the art gallery? Den says they
still have some of your paintings on display."

She smiled at him. "Of course."

"What about misery guts?" Henry ventured. "Will she
be coming with us?"

Robin shook her head. "She says she's working. I'll stay
here as well. The bike needs some tuning up, but I'm sure Jo
would join you."

"Can we take the Jeep?" Paul asked. "I've always
wanted a ride in one."

"You could drive it, if you like," Ellie offered with a
smile.

"I don't drive."

"What! Not at all?" Robin sounded incredulous.

"Never got a license. I don't need to drive, living in London."

"And he's got me to take him places," Henry added. "That's why he keeps me around."

Paul punched him on the arm. "Yes, my own personal chauffeur."

Henry laughed. "Right, well, I'm going in to see if I can pry Den away from her laptop. She needs to be out here getting some fresh air."

"Good luck with that," Robin said. "She was typing away like anything last time I checked."

†

It was all going according to plan. Robin smiled to herself as she listened to Ellie and Jo enthuse about the trip to Hebden Bridge over dinner. The boys also seemed keen on the trip, a Sunday outing, especially as they were going in the Jeep. Den had told her how twitchy Henry was about his car getting damaged.

Once the others had gone and she had planted the idea in Den's mind that she should take a look at Ellie's painting in the studio, Robin would take off on the bike. Kathryn's text indicated she would be arriving about noon.

Den hardly said a word during the meal. When Henry and Paul started on the topic of the exhibition, Robin changed the subject, teasing Jo about her relationship with Ash.

"It's not a relationship. We've only been out for dinner once."

"Well, if you're going to date a cop, you'll have to get rid of you know what."

"I don't actually have any right now." Jo gave her a meaningful look. "You helped me smoke the last one."

"Oh yeah. I forgot."

Jo turned the tables on her, telling everyone how Robin had frightened the cats by jumping up on the coffee table, strumming air guitar and belting out "House of the Rising Sun," at the top of her voice.

"Where was I?" Ellie asked. "I don't remember that."

"I think you were at the gallery," Jo said.

"And I thought you hated that song, Rob."

"Well, she knows all the words," Jo smirked.

"Hey, I was stoned. It's probably a subconscious memory."

At least this conversation brought Den out of her funk long enough to say, "I would've liked to see that."

"You wouldn't have wanted to hear it," Jo said firmly. "The cats had the right idea, running for cover. I found them cowering in the bedroom closet."

When dinner was over, the boys prevailed on Jo to play a some tunes on the guitar. They tried to encourage Robin to do an encore performance but she declined. Jo serenaded them with her soothing renditions of a few mellow folk songs before they all headed off to bed.

During the evening, Robin's own mind was less than tranquil. The thought of seeing Kathryn again was troubling, even though she'd invited her and the encounter was likely to be brief. Through all her numerous affairs, before she came to her senses and committed herself to Ellie, no other woman had made love to her. That part of her was something she only shared with Ellie. The thought that she and the professor had enjoyed that level of intimacy made Robin feel ill. It was the feeling that made her want to kick Kathryn in the groin every time she saw her.

She was doing it for Den, she reminded herself as she finally drifted off to sleep.

Chapter Five

The drive to Ed's house hadn't taken long even though she left Durham later than planned, risking hitting more traffic on the road. Kathryn intended taking the kitten to the RSPCA first thing on Saturday morning but she spent all day enjoying its company, plus a good part of Sunday morning playing with it and laughing at its antics. When she finally left it with the young woman at the animal shelter, she had found herself saying that if no one claimed it she would be happy to take it home again.

Ed was washing his car in the driveway when she drove up. She smiled to herself. Anthropologists of the future would have fun working out this Sunday morning tradition. Men up and down the country were engaged in the same activity, possibly all at the same time. Ed disappeared around the side of the garage as she got out of her car, to switch off the water, she assumed.

He waved to her from the corner, and she followed him around to the back of the house. They entered the kitchen together and he went over to the sink to wash his hands.

"Coffee's on," he said. "Help yourself and pour one for me, too."

She poured the coffees and placed the mugs on the kitchen table, seating herself so she had a view of the garden. Some greenery remained with the large evergreen trees at the back and in the hedge that separated the garden from the neighbor's.

"So, what brings you back to these parts. Can't stay away?" Ed dried his hands on a tea towel and joined her.

She had only told him there was something she needed to check out when she called on Friday evening.

"I'm going up to Starling Hill."

"Oh?"

"It's not what you think. Robin phoned, which is unusual in itself." She related the conversation to Ed.

He sat back and drank some of his coffee before responding. "A public burial. I can't see it being a funeral cortege. It's not like she was hugely popular."

"Neither was Richard III, but the people of Leicester are giving him a big send off. And that's the thing. From what Den tells me, the queen has a massive following on Facebook. She's now a gay icon."

"I'd heard something about that. Hasn't someone set up a fake Twitter account for her as well?"

"Yes, and for Vellocatus."

"You know, that is something I find hard to fathom."

"What's that?" Kathryn knew what he was going to say.

"How did Vee manage to pass as a man? I mean, Roman life, particularly amongst soldiers, was very open. We know what their toilet and bathing arrangements were. They got naked with each other all the time."

"It would have been difficult, but I guess it's something we'll never know. She didn't leave a diary. There's a good chance people did know but maybe she had proved herself to be a good warrior."

"Oh, come on! I know her bones show wounds that would have been inflicted from hard fighting, but the Romans expected their women to be...well, women."

"Yes, but they weren't living in Rome."

"Ah, well," he sat back and finished his coffee. "As you say, I guess we'll never know." He waved his mug. "Another cuppa?"

"Thanks."

He waited until he was sitting down again before asking, "So, how's Denise?"

"I don't know."

He raised an eyebrow and waited for her to continue.

"She took off down to London and I haven't spoken to her since. And, yes, I have phoned but she's ignoring my calls."

"You two both looked great at the opening of the exhibition and that's only a week ago."

Kathryn held out her hand. "She asked me to marry her. This is the engagement ring."

Ed looked at it. "Looks like a family heirloom. I guess you're honored."

"I just…I can't…"

"You can't, what? It's obvious to me, and anyone who sees you two together, that she adores you. It's not still about Eleanor Winters, is it?"

"No, it's…I don't know…maybe it is." Kathryn couldn't meet his gaze.

"Well, I think you need to make your mind up. And in case you hadn't noticed, Eleanor's taken. She and Robin seem pretty tight."

"Yes, I know that."

He invited her to stay for lunch but she wanted to get to the farm, check out the painting, and be on her way back to Durham before dark. Thanking him for the coffee, she headed up into the hills. Replaying their conversation, she hoped she could get through the next visit without making a fool of herself.

†

Glad to be alone when the others drove off, Den stretched and closed her laptop. Robin had given up trying to talk to her as well and went off on her bike. Before she left though, she suggested Den have a look at Ellie's painting. It was, according to Ellie, the place where Cartimandua wanted to be re-buried.

Robin was worried about her partner. Even through her own misery, Den could sense her friend's distress. Robin was always a bit hyperactive, but she had been particularly antsy since Den's arrival.

She decided a walk would be a good idea. As soon as she got to her feet, Harry lifted his head. "Guess we could both do with some fresh air," she said, and he gave his panting agreement.

The dog scampered across the yard while Den stood on the steps outside the house and took a deep breath. The sunshine had taken the edge off the cold start to the morning. She pulled her jacket closed and, hands in pockets, started to walk across to the studio. She heard the sound of a vehicle approaching before she reached the barn.

It was a red car, and as it got closer, Den thought she was hallucinating. It couldn't be, but it was: the professor's Honda Civic.

Kathryn's look of surprise no doubt matched her own. Den watched her lover climb slowly out of the vehicle.

"What are you doing here?" she asked, unable to keep the raw emotion out of her voice.

"I might ask you the same thing," Kathryn replied, the coolness of her tone matching the sharp October air.

Den swallowed hard and shrugged. "Going to look at a painting."

"Ah. That makes sense." Without waiting for Den to respond, Kathryn moved past her and opened the door to the studio.

Shaking her head, Den inhaled another deep breath and let it out slowly as she followed. When she reached Ellie's work area, Kathryn was staring, not at the painting on the easel but at the framed picture on the ledge nearby.

"Where did she get this?"

"I gather Ed sent it to her."

"Robin says she talks to the queen and claims Cazza is speaking to her."

Suddenly Den understood. This explained Robin's behavior since her arrival at the farm. She had planned this, including Henry and Paul's visit, with more tactical sense than Den would have credited her with.

"When did you talk to Robin?"

"She called me on Friday. At the university."

"Must really be worried about Ellie."

Kathryn turned her attention to the painting. They looked at it together.

"Do you know where it is?" asked Den.

"Hard to tell. The two most likely places from what's known of her life would be York or Aldborough."

"Well, that doesn't look anything like York."

"No. But it would have looked a lot different in her day. A settlement of wattle and daub houses clustered near the river. My money would be on Aldborough though." Kathryn turned to her, blue eyes unfocused behind her glasses.

116

They stood facing each other. As usual, Den was finding it hard to gauge Kathryn's mood. The professor broke the silence after a few minutes.

"Den. I'm sorry. This marriage thing. It's going to take me some time to get used to the idea. I just never thought this was something I would have to even consider. I always thought it was one of the bonuses of being a lesbian. And now, just because we can, it doesn't mean we have to. Lots of straight couples just live together…"

"I know. I never thought about getting married before either. When it wasn't an option, I didn't think it was important."

"What's changed?"

"I've met someone I want to spend the rest of my life with, and I want people to know. To show the world that our relationship is just as valid as anyone else's."

Kathryn twisted the ring off her finger. "I want to be with you, Den. But we both know I'm not ready for this step. Take this and ask me again at Christmas, if you still want to by then, that is."

Den tucked the ring away to an inside pocket of her jacket. She pulled Kathryn close and whispered, "I will always want you." Their lips met and Den was overwhelmed by the intensity of Kathryn's response, her teeth opening to accept her tongue.

The sound of the barn door opening startled them both.

†

This is nuts, Ash whispered to herself as she turned up the lane. *I'm on duty, but I just want to see her again.*

Jo's van was parked up alongside the Corsa. The bike was missing but there were two cars she hadn't seen before—a white BMW and a red Honda Civic—both a bit upmarket for this dyke commune. She parked the police car next to the Honda and put her hat on as she got out, ingrained habit. Also out of habit, she clocked the registration numbers on the strange cars

Ash knocked on the farmhouse door before entering. In the middle of the day on a Sunday, there should be someone around, but the silence in the house was clear evidence no one was home. One of the cats, Soames she thought, was making himself at home on the otherwise empty sofa, stretched out to his full length. He didn't acknowledge her presence. Ash went outside and peered into the windows of the van.

Harry appeared and, unlike the cat, greeted her enthusiastically. She stroked his head, thoughtfully. He was proof that someone was here, probably Jo. Most likely in the barn.

The sight that greeted her when she opened the door was unexpected. Two women she hadn't seen before were making out. She would have backed out gracefully without disturbing them, but then her radio crackled into life, giving away her presence.

The women broke apart and stared at her. The taller one immediately put her hands up in the air in surrender.

Ash silenced her radio. *Probably just her partner checking when she was picking him up.* "I'm looking for Jo Bright Flame. Is she here?"

The tall one brought her hands down to her sides. "No. She's gone over to Hebden with the others. I think they're planning on having lunch there."

"Okay. Thanks. Sorry to disturb you. As you were." She gave them a mock salute, pivoted on her heel and walked out. *Phew! Definitely something in the air here. Time to get back to the real world.*

She had reached her car and opened the door when another noise distracted her. Coming up the track was a tour bus. Ash recalled the discussion the last time she was at the farm when a coach of sightseers arrived. She could understand why Ellie Winters was disturbed by the unwanted intrusion into her peaceful way of life. Starling Hill was hardly on the way to anywhere. You didn't "just pass" here.

The motorbike roared up behind the coach and barely came to a standstill before an angry Robin leapt off it. She was removing her helmet and ready to launch into a fight with the young man who emerged from the bus. Deciding she needed to step in, Ash pulled her notebook out of her pocket with a practiced move and stepped between the two would-be combatants.

"Name," she said brusquely to the tour guide.

He looked completely taken aback. "Um…I…"

"That was the easy one, sunshine. The hard questions come later."

The young man gulped. "We're just here to look at the field."

"You are aware this is private land."

"Yes, but…"

"But, do you have the landowner's permission?" Ash made a show of writing in her notebook.

"I, um, don't know. I'm just the guide."

"Well, I suggest you get back in your nice bus and take your tourists somewhere else. I've noted your presence on this occasion, so tell your bosses to get their ducks in a row before you make any more trips up here. Do I make myself clear?"

The red-faced youngster nodded and climbed back inside the coach. Ash motioned to Robin to move out of the way. They watched the bus driver negotiate a difficult three-point turn before heading the coach back down the lane.

"That was awesome." Robin grinned at her. "Thanks, Ash. What are you doing here, anyway?"

"Just called by to see Jo before starting my shift."

"Oh right. Well, they won't be back for a while."

"Okay. Um, I'll phone her later." Ash removed her hat and got back into the car. She rolled down the window. "Maybe you should see about getting that gate."

Robin nodded and waved her off.

In her rearview mirror she saw the other two women had come out of the barn, holding hands. She wondered who they were. Maybe she could do a sneaky PNC check on the registration numbers of the two unfamiliar vehicles. On the other hand, she could just ask Jo when she saw her again. And she definitely wanted to see her again.

†

Kathryn and Den had emerged from the barn in time to witness the cop's confrontation with the young man from the coach. Watching the departure of first the coach and then the police car, Kathryn turned to Den, "Coach tour?"

"Looks like it. That won't go down too well with Ellie, I shouldn't think."

"No. Why would they come all the way up here to look at an empty field?"

"Who knows? Guess the exhibition generated a lot of interest."

Robin joined them.

"Did you see the guy's face? Priceless! That should be the last we see of them."

"Yeah. Why are the police interested in Jo?"

"Only one police officer is interested in Jo." Robin laughed. "They've had one dinner date and it looks like Ash is already angling for another. Anyway, would you two like something to drink?"

"No thanks." Kathryn turned to Den. "I'd like to get off now."

"Okay. I'll collect my stuff. Won't be long."

Kathryn watched her go into the house before turning to Robin. "I always thought you were a devious little shit and my opinion hasn't changed. But I suppose I should thank you."

"You're welcome. And I don't like you any more than I did before, but Den seems quite taken with you for some reason. No accounting for taste. Anyway, Den's a mate, so do you think you could try a bit harder to make her happy?"

"Like you're qualified to be giving relationship advice."

Robin gave her a lopsided grin. "Doing better than you so far."

"It's not a competition."

Den came out of the house with her backpack slung over her shoulder.

"Maybe not." Kathryn managed a proper smile.

"So, what did you think of the painting?" Robin asked.

"It could be anywhere in the north."

"According to Ellie, the queen calls it 'Old Barrow'."

"Most likely somewhere around Aldborough, then."

Den put her bag in the boot of Kathryn's car and joined them. "How does Ellie communicate with Cazza? I mean, she wouldn't have spoken English, not as we know it, anyway."

"Yeah, I asked her that." Robin looked over at the field. "She says they use a sort of pidgin Latin. Ellie studied Latin for a few years and Cartimandua picked up the language from her contact with the Romans." Robin shuffled her feet before looking back at Kathryn. "Look, I know this sounds weird, but it's like she's having real conversations. Cartimandua said she wants a proper state funeral. Ellie told her that would cost a lot of money. And guess what? The queen said, no problem. She can pay for it. They stashed a load of coins here."

"What! Where? We didn't find anything much. Some bling…torques, armbands, remnants of Vee's armor. The few coins we found were from after her time."

"That's the problem. Vee hid it…in case they were ever discovered."

"Has Vee told Ellie where it is?" Kathryn couldn't quite believe they were talking about this as if it were real.

"Vee doesn't 'talk' to her. Cartimandua says she'll ask. But anyway, Jo has a friend who's got a top of the range metal detector. She's going to talk to him about coming over."

Kathryn looked at Den, then back to Robin. "I'd like to be here when he does it."

"Sure. I'll let you know when they've set up a time. It'll probably be the weekend anyway."

"I can see why she's worried about Ellie," Den said as they set off. "You don't really believe there's any buried treasure here, do you?"

Kathryn maneuvered her car carefully down the rutted track, waiting until they were safely on the smoother road surface before replying.

"It's something that puzzled us during the dig. We knew that it was likely she had to leave without taking many possessions, but she was in power for a long time. Trade with the Romans was a lucrative business. People may not have liked her politics, but she knew how to make money. We thought she must have brought some with her."

"So, why didn't you use a metal detector during the dig?"

Kathryn gave her a quick sideways glance before returning her attention to the narrow road. "Metal detecting is not archaeology."

"Oh, yeah, sorry. Silly me."

Archaeologists regarded treasure hunters with disdain. A fact Kathryn knew Den was well aware of. She sincerely hoped Robin wouldn't conveniently forget to let her know when Jo's friend came by. If there was a hoard to be discovered she wanted to be on hand to make sure no archaeology was destroyed in the process of digging it up.

†

Henry watched Paul's delight while Ellie showed him her paintings. He joined them as Paul was enthusing about the colors and the way the clouds seemed to move across the sky in one of the pictures.

"Is it for sale?" he asked.

"Yes, it is," Ellie said, turning her radiant smile on him. "But I have some others at home that haven't been put on display yet."

"I love this one. Could we buy it, Hen?"

Paul knew how to push his buttons and that Henry wasn't likely to refuse him. Certainly not in a public place.

Ellie was looking embarrassed.

"Please. I didn't bring you here to make you buy my work. As I said, I have some completed canvases at home, which I think you'll like just as well. And I would be happy to give you one."

Ellie's generosity was something Henry realized was a completely natural part of her. The offer was genuine but he couldn't accept it.

"That's extremely kind of you, Ellie. But if Paul's taken a fancy to this one, we'll have to buy it."

She bit her lip and looked back and forth between them. "Well, if you're sure, I'll ask Helen to give you a discount."

"You don't need to do that. I'm happy to pay the full price."

She touched his arm and Henry felt the jolt of desire that had surfaced when he first met Ellie. Women didn't normally affect him this way.

"Friends get a discount. No arguments, please." She withdrew her hand and he felt the loss of contact immediately. "I'll go and talk to Helen."

She walked off to find the gallery owner and Henry glanced up to find Paul looking at him with an impish grin on his face.

"You going het on me, Hen?"

"I don't know what you mean."

"Sure you do. I recognize that lustful look in your eyes. But I understand. If anyone could turn a guy straight, it would be her."

"It's a passing fancy. And anyway, Robin would kill me."

"True enough. These dykes get mightily possessive. Jas told me that Robin and Steph looked like they were squaring off in the kitchen the other day. It would be a tough one to call. Steph's got the muscle but I reckon Robin's a scrapper."

Henry laughed. Ellie returned with the French woman in tow. She introduced them and ten minutes later they were walking out of the gallery, Paul carrying the wrapped painting. After placing it carefully in the back of the Jeep, Ellie suggested they walk over to the cafe where they were meeting Jo. There was no point moving the car. All available parking spaces would have been taken up by now—Henry had been fortunate to find one in the town center.

†

The town's population seemed to double at weekends. Visitors of all shapes and sizes filled the streets, wandering aimlessly, enjoying the sunshine. Ducks swarmed over the stone steps by the old packhorse bridge, anticipating treats from the many passers-by.

Jo smiled at the street performer. He often stopped to chat with her when she was on her stall. Days like this were a bonus for him; his hat was filling up with coins. The sun brought out smiles and an expansion in people's hearts.

Jo had taken a nostalgic trip along the canal towpath, stopping at the place Molly's boat had been moored. There was another boat there now, an old clunker that was being given a new lease on life. That seemed like a good metaphor for her own feelings. Was she ready to take on the challenge of a new relationship? Her thoughts strayed to the evening spent with the police officer. Ash's hair looked like it was just growing back in. Was she a cancer survivor? Jo realized that their conversation hadn't really touched on anything too deep. Maybe Ash wasn't ready for anything more either. She hadn't called, so it didn't look like Jo was going to get the chance to find out.

Further on from the old boat, she found Jed's barge, a bright medley of colors adorning the cabin's exterior. Some evergreen plants were still thriving on the roof. The name, *Mystic Dawn*, had always appealed to her.

The curtains were drawn on each of the vessel's small windows, but Jo knocked on the one by the stern anyway.

"Looking for Jed, love?" A voice called out.

Jo saw someone on a neighboring boat waving. She walked over so the woman didn't have to shout.

"Yes. He doesn't usually sleep this late."

"Well, he's not there. Gone over to his daughter's in Skipton and won't be back for a fortnight. I'm keeping an eye on things for him."

"Oh, right. Fine. I'll catch up with him later. I'm Jo, from the market."

"Of course. I thought I'd seen you around."

Jo walked back into town. It was time to meet up with the others. She was going to have to tell Ellie that Jed and his metal detector weren't available, at least not for the next two weeks.

†

Ellie let Henry drive the Jeep back to the farm, sitting in the back with Jo. Whatever Robin's intentions, having a break from the farm had been a good idea. She was feeling more relaxed than she had for days. Conversations with the queen were often intense, trying to explain how different things were in the twenty-first century. And then there was the problem of trying to convince anyone else that the queen and her consort deserved a proper burial. Ellie only had a vague idea that the Ministry of Justice needed to be involved. Although maybe not for a two thousand year old skeleton. Cartimandua hadn't been a Christian so there was no need for her to be buried in consecrated ground.

Talking to Kathryn would be the obvious answer. Ever since their last conversation in the summer when it was clear the professor was still harboring feelings for her, Ellie had avoided contact. Using Ed McLaughlin as an intermediary was the likely scenario.

Finding the coins was another problem. Jo's friend wasn't available to help out. Ellie hadn't been sure about asking an outsider anyway. She did know that when valuable hoards were found, the finder would get a percentage. If there was any way to give the queen and her lover a ceremonial send off, she was sure all the money would be needed to offset the cost.

The Frome hoard, found a few years earlier, contained 52,000 coins dating from the latter part of the third century, and had been valued at over three hundred thousand pounds. Depending on whether or not the queen's treasure chest consisted of mainly gold and silver, it could be valued at a lot more. A hoard found at nearby Honley in 1893 was all silver, but there had been one with an image of a woman, possibly Cartimandua. Other coins from that collection featured two men thought to be her father and brother. But their names, Volisios and Dunmocveros sounded more Roman than British. So little was known about Cartimandua that a find which could shed more light on her life would be of great historical interest. Everything written about that time was from the Roman viewpoint, and even that was written many years later.

Jo touched her arm. "Are you okay, Ellie?"

"Yes." She smiled at her. "Just thinking. I've really enjoyed today."

"Good. When we get back, I need to talk to you about the pottery classes."

"Sure." With the events of the past week, Ellie had forgotten about the upcoming classes. She and Kieran had been running them for years during the winter months, but Kieran was in Australia so Ellie had asked Jo to take it on. She would help out when she could but planned to leave it mainly to Jo. And it would give Jo some income. Although they hadn't discussed it Ellie knew Jo was worried about paying her way at the farm. They hadn't asked her for rent, but she helped out with food costs when she could.

When they arrived, Robin was sitting on the step outside the house with Harry at her feet. They looked at peace. Harry jumped to his feet though and was on Paul as soon as he got out of the Jeep.

"Looks like you're his new best friend." Jo laughed.

"Might have been the bacon I slipped him at breakfast."

"That will do it."

Robin got up more slowly than Harry and joined the group.

"All quiet here?" Henry asked.

"Yeah. Well, apart from the coach arriving."

"What!" Ellie was shocked.

Robin put her arm around her shoulders. "It's okay. They were put off by the presence of a police car and a cop in uniform. She gave them a warning."

"She…oh, you mean, Ash. What was she doing here?"

"Looking for someone, I think?" Robin said with a straight face, winking at Jo, who blushed furiously.

Ellie glanced around. "Where's Den? She's not still cooped up inside, is she?"

"Um, no. Actually, she's gone back to Durham."

"Oh. You took her to the train station. That's good."

"Not exactly." Robin let go of her and started to walk back towards the house. Ellie caught up before she reached the door.

"What do you mean?"

"Well, Kathryn turned up. They seemed keen to have a reunion."

Ellie gave her lover a searching look. "Just what have you been up to?"

Robin shrugged. "Nothing."

"I know that look. You're going to come upstairs and tell me everything." Ellie turned to the group still clustered around the Jeep with Harry. "Help yourselves to something to drink. Rob and I have something to discuss."

She thought she heard Henry say, "Is that what you call it?" before she dragged Robin into the house.

†

They hadn't talked much on the drive back to Durham. Kathryn concentrated on driving and Den watched the cars passing and the glimpses of scenery.

There was no conversation when they arrived at the flat. Den pushed Kathryn against the wall by the door and deftly removed her glasses before kissing her. The professor didn't protest as she unzipped her trousers and slipped her hand through. The wetness that met Den's hand did surprise her.

"It's a wonder we got here in one piece if this is what you were thinking about," Den whispered.

Kathryn moaned, "Don't talk. Just take me to bed."

If they weren't upright in a most uncomfortable position, Den would have thought she was dreaming when she heard those words. She didn't need any further encouragement and the next few hours were spent exploring each other's bodies. Den's only coherent thought during that time was that if getting unengaged had this effect on her lover, they would have to do it on a regular basis.

A duet of rumbling stomachs reminded them that they hadn't had eaten any food since breakfast. Den propped herself up on one elbow and looked into Kathryn's unfocused blue eyes.

"How about a shower?"

"If you're suggesting we do it together, we won't get anything to eat for another hour."

Den refrained from stating the obvious. "Is there any food in the house?"

"Frozen pizza."

"That'll do. You shower first, I'll put the oven on." Den kissed her forehead and climbed out of bed. Their clothes were scattered throughout the flat. She followed the trail to find all the items she needed. Tripping over a box on the kitchen floor she let out a yell.

Kathryn came in, wrapped in a towel. "What's the matter?"

"This." It looked like a box of sand, half the contents now spread out over the tiles. "What the fuck is it?"

"Oh."

"Oh, what?"

Kathryn moved closer and looked up, a goofy smile on her face. "How would you feel about adopting a kitten?"

"Are you serious?"

"Yes." Kathryn told her about finding the small creature crouching by the door in the rain. "I've offered to take her if no one makes a claim. Her name's Misty. I think you'll like her."

"If she's a stray, how do you know she's called Misty? Or did she tell you that?" Den had spent part of the time on the drive home thinking about Ellie's supposed conversations with the long dead Cartimandua.

"No. That's what I named her. She's mostly grey with a bit of white on her chest and her paws."

Den smiled at her. "You've become all maternal. I think I like it."

"But, really, are you okay with it? You're not allergic or anything, are you?"

"No. You do realize this fulfills a typical lesbian stereotype."

Kathryn just gave her an enigmatic smile and drifted off to the bathroom.

After switching the oven on, Den cleared up the mess on the floor with the brush and pan. She washed her hands before removing the pizza from the freezer and unwrapping it. Pouring two glasses of red wine, she carried them into the living room and sat down. The river flowed muddily past, and as she watched the swirls and eddies, Den thought the moment couldn't get any better. Quite a change from her early morning despondency.

†

Robin let Ellie pull her into the house. She followed her meekly up the stairs to their bedroom. Once inside, Ellie pushed her down onto the bed.

"I've missed you too, hon." Robin started to undo the buttons on her shirt.

Ellie raised a hand to stop her. "No you don't. You're not distracting me. Why was Kathryn here? You called her, didn't you?"

"Yes."

"Why?"

Robin patted the bed beside her. "Come and sit down, love. I can't talk to you while you're doing your teacher number on me."

When Ellie was seated, Robin took her hand in hers. "Look, you know I've been worried. All this stuff with you and Cartimandua. I can't get my head around it. But I thought, well, if anyone can make sense of it, Kathryn can. If you and queenie are serious about this re-burial thing then she'll know who needs to organize it. You can't just go around burying old bones in someone else's field. The professor had a look at the painting and is willing to check out some locations."

"That's all very well, sweetheart. But you should have told me. And I suppose Kathryn now thinks I'm going off my head as well."

Robin looked into Ellie's eyes and saw the moisture gathering. "Hey, I'm sorry. I didn't want to upset you. No one thinks you're crazy. Well, maybe a little. But, honestly, Kathryn's taking it seriously. She said she wants to be here when Jo's friend comes over with his metal detector."

"Oh." Ellie brushed at her face. Her cheeks were wet, but she wasn't crying. "He's away and won't be able to come for a few weeks."

"Okay. Well, maybe that's for the best. We can always hire a detector ourselves if we want to give it a go."

"You do believe me, don't you?" Ellie's eyes were still watery.

Robin smiled and hugged her close. "Yes, I do. We're in this together."

The radiant smile that lit up Ellie's features when she said this was worth more than any amount of hidden treasure.

Ellie kissed her deeply. When their lips parted for air, she whispered, "I love you."

Robin felt those words rip through to her core. She wanted to act on it, but knew this wasn't the time. "Hold that thought, Miss Winters. I think we should go see what our guests are up to. We don't want them to feel neglected."

Ellie's eyes now held a promise that Robin knew would be fulfilled later when they were alone.

Chapter Six

A late start on a Monday morning was an unusual luxury for Steph, although sleeping was not first and foremost on her mind. Waking up at her normal time simply meant she had several hours to enjoy giving Jasmine her full attention.

They had the house to themselves as Henry and Paul were still up north and not due back until the evening. After a leisurely breakfast and a second cup of coffee, Steph enticed Jas into the living room and they had made love on the sofa.

Steph smiled as she parked her van on the quiet residential street by Holland Park. It had been a memorable morning so far and it was only half past ten. She walked across the road to the large terraced house with the wisteria vine looming around the doorframe. That would need cutting back for a start. Getting a gig in this part of town would pay well and give her the funds to treat Jas to a weekend away in a country house hotel.

The door opened before she could lift the ostentatious brass knocker and she found herself gazing at what could only be described as a large pair of "knockers." Looking up she saw an amused smirk on the face of the attractive blonde holding the door open.

"Ah, the gardener. Please come in." She stood aside leaving just enough room for Steph to move past her crabwise, narrowly avoiding contact with the protruding breasts. The woman's skimpy outfit didn't leave anything to the imagination.

"Follow me."

Steph wasn't an art connoisseur but she could see there were some valuable pieces hanging on the walls. Before they reached the end of the wide hall, they came to a short flight of steps leading to a small door. She followed the blonde out into the garden.

The variety of plants wouldn't have looked out of place in Kew Gardens. It wasn't a large area but it was stuffed with a lot of greenery including a six-foot-high conifer hedge along one side.

"We've let it get a bit out of hand, as you can see. Everything needs cutting back."

"Yes."

"So, as I mentioned on the phone, we would like a quote for the work that needs doing."

"Okay."

"Right-o. I'll leave you to it. Just give me a shout when you're done."

Steph watched her leave, a comely sight from behind as well. *Get your mind on the job, Stephanie,* she admonished herself, pulling her notebook out of her pocket. She walked down to the end of the garden to look inside the gazebo. It was covered in wisteria as well. To the side was a small pond with two fat looking Koi swimming around, possibly looking for a way out.

Her phone buzzed. Steph looked at the screen and grinned. Only gone half an hour and her love was missing her already. "Hey, babe."

"Hey yourself. Look, I thought if you're not digging anything up, we could meet for lunch in town."

"Hm. Not a bad idea. I'm just doing a quote at a house near Holland Park. In fact, I think it probably backs onto the park." Steph sat down in the gazebo and looked back at the house. She didn't think she was being observed but best not to spend too long chatting.

"Holland Park?"

"Yeah. Well, the address is actually Kensington. Probably owned by some Russian oligarch. The busty blonde who opened the door looked like the kind of trophy wife they usually have hanging off their arms."

"What's her name?"

"Jeez, I don't know. I think she said Rosy, or something like that.

"What's the house number?" Jas sounded odd.

"Um. Seventeen."

"Fuck. I knew it. She hasn't let go."

"Jas…"

"That's Max's house. The blonde's her PA, Roisin. Just get out of there. Please, Steph. Now." The panic in Jas's voice was unmistakable.

"Right. Okay." Steph ended the call and sat for a moment before deciding what to do. She walked slowly, looking around and glancing at her notebook, in case she was being watched. There was only one way out, through the house. She walked quickly down the long hallway and opened the front door. The blonde met her coming up the steps.

"Are you finished already?"

"Yes, it's not a big job. I'll get the quote to you tomorrow."

"When would you be able to start?"

"I've got a few jobs on this week. Would next Monday be okay?" Steph hoped she sounded calmer than she felt.

"Good-o. That's great. Nice to meet you."

"Yeah. Thanks." Steph walked across to her van resisting the urge to run. The woman was watching on the steps of the house and, as she pulled away, Steph thought she could see Roisin taking out a phone to make a call.

She set off back towards Chiswick and was halfway there when a thought occurred to her. What was Roisin doing outside? It wasn't the kind of neighborhood where they had milk delivered. What if this was all a trick to lead

Max Fleetwood straight to Jas? Instead of taking the turn off leading to Henry's house, she carried on down the Great West Road and didn't look for a place to park until she reached Hounslow. Finding a quiet street, she got out of the van and checked each of the wheel arches. Sure enough, there was something attached to the front right one. It had to be a tracking device. Steph removed it and placed it on the low wall in front of the small terraced house she'd stopped outside.

Driving home, she smiled grimly to herself. It was only delaying the inevitable. If Max knew her name and mobile number, and the PA had no doubt noted her van registration, she would have the means to track down her address. Disregarding all speed limits, Steph raced back home. The jobs she did have lined up for the week could all be put off. It might be a good idea if she and Jas disappeared for a while.

†

The morning started off well. Where nothing had gone right on Friday, everything was falling into place now. Responses to her previous emails were coming in and Den had enough work to keep busy for a few weeks.

She couldn't quite believe the change in Kathryn. Released from their brief engagement, Kathryn was relaxed and happy and had gone off to work with a smile on her face after their early morning love making. Den gave the sapphire ring one last lingering glance as she placed it in its box and returned it to the back of her desk drawer.

The call from Jas came just as she was finishing her second cup of coffee.

"I knew it," Jas didn't bother with a greeting. "She won't let go."

Den had a good idea what she was talking about. "What's happened?"

Jas told her about Steph's narrow escape.

"A tracking device! You're kidding me. Does she think she's with MI5?"

"It's no joke, Den."

"Yeah, I know. Look, it's in hand. I don't think you'll have to worry about her much longer."

"She could turn up here any minute."

"Will you just calm down and listen? Do you remember Fiery Fitz?"

"Marsha Fitzwilliam. Yes, of course."

"And you know she writes a gossip column for a certain paper?"

"Yes, so? How does this help get Max off my back, so to speak."

"After we talked last week, I contacted her." They had gone to school with Fitz. When Den and Jas started up a school newspaper, Fitz had helped them out and always seemed to know who to tap up for the best stories. "There will be something in her piece today. No names, but Ms. Fleetwood will get the message."

"How do we know Max will see it?"

"One of Fitz's colleagues will be ringing her up to ask if she would like to comment on it."

"No shit! Wow! Den, you're the best."

"Well, yeah, I know." Den could hear the relief in Jasmine's voice.

"I can't thank you and Fitz enough."

"Hey, Fitz was only too happy to run something on Max. It's something she's wanted to do for years but couldn't get a handle on her."

After more effusive thanks from Jas with Steph joining in from the background, Den went back to the research she'd started on reinterment. The most recent example was that of Richard III. She would ask Kathryn if she had a contact at the University of Leicester. Plans for reburial would be well underway now that the decision had been taken to bury the former king with honors at Leicester Cathedral. It seemed there was some sort of legal requirement to make sure his remains were interred as near as possible to where his bones had been discovered.

Den wondered if this would apply to Cartimandua. She didn't think Ellie would be happy with a shrine to the Queen of the Brigantes on her land. Also, the church wouldn't need to be involved. Cazza had been a tribal chief, not an anointed monarch. What kind of ceremony would she have? The Druids were the main force in terms of any kind of organized religion in her time. Den had no doubt the modern day Druids would be thrilled to have a chance to perform a ritual over the dead queen and her lover. She wasn't sure what their stand on lesbianism was, but it was likely to be more liberal than most of the Christian churches.

†

It had been a dull morning only brightened in Ash's mind by the chat she'd had with Jo the night before. When she finally worked up the courage to call, Jo had accepted her invitation to dinner at her house on Tuesday evening. She had been so relieved by Jo's positive response that she almost forgot to ask her about the two strange women at the farm.

"I thought you might be making pots, so I went into the studio and found two women making out."

"Oh, that was Den and the professor. Den came up from London with Henry and Paul. And Dr. Moss had come over from Durham to look at Ellie's painting."

Apart from Ellie, the names meant nothing to Ash. "Sounds complicated. You'll have to fill me in on Tuesday."

Ash's daydreaming was disturbed by a call on the radio. Since she was driving her partner answered. A jeweler's had been held up and the robbers were making their getaway in a gray Nissan Micra.

Ross gave her a sideways glance. "Stupid fuckers. Who picks a Micra as a getaway car?" He told the dispatcher they were good to respond. "Hit the gas, Ash. We can intercept them before they reach the motorway."

Ash liked working with Ross. He always let her drive and kept his sexist comments to himself. Now he slapped the dashboard with his hands. "Come on Ash, this is definitely a GLF road." He put the siren and flashers on.

GLF was their acronym for "go like fuck" and Ash was only too happy to comply, catching sight of worried looking drivers as she weaved past their cars—anxiety turning to relief when they realized the cop car wasn't interested in them.

The day was definitely looking up, and with a glimpse of the fleeing Micra not far ahead, Ash gave herself to the thrill of the chase.

In the end it was the perps who lost their nerve and obligingly pulled over to the side of the road. A second police car arrived from the other direction before Ross and Ash had time to get out of their vehicle with their hats on.

"Good work, mate," one of the other officers said to Ross when they had the two scared looking boys secured in the back of their car.

"I wasn't driving. She was."

"Oh, right." He gave Ash a brief nod, then looked at Ross again. "You don't mind if we take over from here. We've been after these two for some time."

"No problem. All yours."

When they were back in their car and driving off, Ross muttered, "Arseholes. They're welcome to the paperwork."

Ash agreed. Making an arrest was all very well, but spending the next few hours filling out forms was the least favorite part of the job. And she was still on an adrenalin high from the chase. She hoped she could hang onto this overwhelming sense of power for the following evening when she would need to have a difficult conversation with Jo.

†

When the call came through on her mobile, Kathryn thought it would be Den, and facing a class full of students she would have to ignore it. Glancing down she saw the caller was the RSPCA.

"Excuse me. I need to take this." She pressed the green button and walked out of the room, closing the door behind her. "Yes."

"The kitten you brought in the other day. She's been checked over. No chip. And no one's contacted us about her being missing, so if you were serious about wanting to take her on, you can collect her anytime. But the sooner the better. We're a bit pushed for space this week."

"No problem." Kathryn ran through the day's schedule in her head. "I can be there by four."

"Lovely, we'll see you then."

Kathryn texted Den quickly before returning to her class. "Misty's coming home. Can you buy cat food?" There were other things they would need. Toys, proper cat litter, and a basket. The latter was important since she wasn't sure how Den would feel about sharing their bed with Misty.

†

The chat with Den had eased Jasmine's worry that Max was going to show up on their doorstep any moment. But Steph was still thinking they should get out of London for a while.

"What about visiting your parents?"

Jas grimaced. "I can only take my mother in small doses. Especially now she's convinced I'm doomed to a life of misery." Jas had finally come out to her parents at her cousin's wedding a little over a month ago, and her mother's reaction to the news had been overwhelmingly negative, although Steph seemed to have bonded with her father during the reception. "Anyway, we'll be going there for Christmas."

"Okay. Why don't we go visit this farm, then? I'd like to see the place, now that I've been to the exhibition."

"I should think they're fed up with visitors. They've had Henry and Paul all weekend."

"We don't need to stay there. After a look around and a cup of tea, we could head on up to Durham. Den's invited us, hasn't she?"

"Yeah, well. Maybe if we stay in a B&B. I think they need their space right now." Jas squeezed her lover's arm. "Are you sure you can take the time off?"

"They're all regular customers. Just a bit of pruning. I'll tell them it's a family emergency."

Jas leant back and let Steph's strong arms enfold her. "Mm. I think a break's a good idea."

†

After one of Ellie's beautifully cooked breakfasts with the boys exclaiming over the wonders of eating fresh farm eggs, they cheerfully waved them off. Robin laughed as she watched Henry trying to carefully navigate the many hazards as he drove down the lane.

"Well, I think they enjoyed themselves," Ellie said.

"Henry says he'll rent a car when they come again. So I guess that means they did." Jo turned to Ellie. "I was going to start setting up the studio for the students. Can you take a look later and make sure I've covered everything?"

Ellie smiled at her. "Yes, of course. I'll be in the studio anyway."

"So, when's the big date?" Robin asked.

"What big date?"

"She did call last night, didn't she?"

Jo felt herself blushing. "Oh, that. Well, tomorrow evening. I'm going to her house for dinner."

"Ooh, romantic."

"She said I could bring Harry."

"No way! You're not taking your dog on a date."

"It's not a date. We're just having a quiet meal together."

"Robin, leave her alone." Ellie gave her partner a stern look. "I thought you were going to Leeds today."

"Okay, fine. I can take a hint." Robin smirked at Jo before going into the house. "Maybe she thinks Harry will protect her from your womanly wiles."

Ellie took Jo's arm as they set off towards the barn together. "Don't mind her. I think it's sweet that Ash wants to include Harry."

Jo wasn't sure how to respond. She had no intention of taking Harry. She was hoping the invitation to Ash's house was an indication of something deeper developing.

†

It was quiet this morning. Ellie wondered if the presence of visitors at the weekend had upset the queen. She hoped not. There were so many things she wanted to ask. Not just about the location of the coins, but more about the queen's life, and her death. The historical notes for the exhibition had been sketchy. Kathryn's archaeology finds had uncovered more questions than the experts had answers for.

Cartimandua was used to being chief of a large tribe. Why did she and her partner settle at Starling Hill? Who else lived with them? There must have been others. She would surely have had servants or loyal retainers who followed her into exile. There was also so much more to learn about Vellocatus. Who was she? Why did she choose to be a warrior? How did she pass as a man?

Ellie's musing was interrupted by the sound of a vehicle arriving in the yard. She went out hoping it wasn't another coach full of sightseers, and it was a relief to see Dr. Ed McLaughlin unfolding his long form out of the Mini Cooper. He caught her amused glance.

"It's the wife's. She needed the Volvo today." He pushed his glasses back up his nose.

"Well, it's good to see you. Thank you so much for the framed photo. It's perfect."

"No problem." He gave her a searching look. "Well, I don't see any outward signs of madness. Kathryn stopped by yesterday. Said you've been talking to Cartimandua."

Ellie sighed. "I guess I have Robin to thank for spreading the word."

"She's only concerned about you."

"I know."

"Anyway, I'd like to see this mysterious painting, if that's all right."

"Of course." Ellie led the way back into her studio. She stood back to let Ed view the canvas in the best light.

He studied it for several minutes before speaking. "I like your landscapes. This wouldn't look out of place on my living room wall." He paused. "It's not anywhere around here though, is it?"

"No."

"What did Kathryn think?"

"I don't know. I wasn't here. She and Den were gone by the time I got back from Hebden Bridge."

"Den was here?"

"Yes. More meddling by Robin. Anyway, they seem to be reconciled for now."

Ed smiled. "That's good news." He took another long look at the image. "I'll ring her later, see if she's had any thoughts. And, regardless of whether I believe the queen told you or not, I think a re-burial is a good idea."

"You do?" Ellie felt suddenly lighter than she had for days. "That's great. She'll be pleased." Catching the return of a frown on Ed's face, she quickly added, "I know you think it's mad, but I really do hear her voice."

"Thankfully we live in enlightened times. They burned Joan of Arc at the stake for claiming God spoke to her."

Ellie's response was interrupted by Robin clattering into the studio wearing her motorcycle gear and carrying her helmet. "Hey, Dr. Ed. Nice wheels."

"I've just got it for the day."

"If I didn't need to rush off I would have loved to take it for a spin. Always fancied one of those." She looked across at Ellie. "Looks like we're in for more visitors, love."

"Oh no! Not another coach?"

"No. Jas phoned. She and Steph are going up to Durham but wanted to break the journey here, just to take a look around."

"Today?"

"No, they'll set off early tomorrow."

"Okay. Good. Can you pick up some chocolate biscuits on your way home?"

"There's still a few left."

"I know, but Ed and I are going in now to have a cup of coffee and we might be inclined to finish them off."

"Okay. I think we're low on milk as well." Robin pulled her into a quick hug and then strode out with a brief wave for Ed.

"So, you've had a full house?"

"Yes. I don't know if you met them at the exhibition. Henry and Paul, Den's housemates in London. Anyway, they left just before you got here."

They started walking towards the house, the sound of Robin's bike receding down the lane.

"Have you heard from Kieran?" Ed asked.

"Yes. He emailed us some photos last night. His grandson's grown, like they do."

"What about your granddaughter? She'll be one soon, won't she? Have you seen her recently?"

"Not in person." Ellie smiled. "We Skype regularly. Aiden promised they'll be with us for Christmas."

Ed stayed for coffee and they sat at the kitchen table talking about nothing in particular and everything in general. The biscuits Ellie put out on a plate disappeared as they chatted.

After the second cup of coffee, Ed said, "Would you be willing to have your DNA tested?"

Ellie thought she'd misheard. "My DNA? Whatever for?"

"Well, I think it's a bit of a long shot, but there is the possibility we could find out if you're related to

Cartimandua. I mean, your family has been here for generations, right?"

"Yes. But not two thousand years. Four hundred is the furthest my dad could trace back."

"It would be difficult to be certain just with the mitochondrial DNA. She didn't have any children that we know of. And there's no definite patrilineal line to verify the findings."

Ellie closed her eyes. Soames had come into the kitchen to investigate when he heard the biscuit tin being opened and was sitting on her lap. She stroked his large ginger head absently. "Did Kathryn put you up to this?" she asked, opening her eyes again to pierce the archaeologist with the gimlet-eyed stare that had always worked on students when she taught history.

"Sort of. I mean, she didn't specifically ask me to ask you. It's a project she wants to set up."

"But, from what you've just said, and also what I've read recently, these tests are pretty meaningless once you go back a few generations. Britain's been invaded so many times since Cartimandua's time, it's pretty safe to say any one of us is descended from Romans, Vikings, Saxons—take your pick. And we all go back to Africa anyway."

"I warned Kathryn it would be a hard sell."

Soames jumped off her lap when he realized there were no biscuits left. Ellie sighed. "Will it cost me anything?"

"I'm sure any costs will be waived if you're willing to be our first victim."

"And no publicity, please. It's bad enough having coach parties turning up to gawk at the field."

"You drive a hard bargain, Ms. Winters, but we will be eternally grateful."

"I suppose you're now going to tell me you just happen to have one of these testing kits on your person."

"In the car, actually."

"You devious sod." Ellie shook her head but gave him a fond smile. "I can't believe I gave you the last of our chocolate biscuits."

†

Who knew that a kitten was all Kathryn really wanted? Den smiled to herself watching the professor who was lying on the living room carpet, pulling the string for Misty to chase. She sipped at her wine and looked again at the laminated photograph Kathryn had brought home along with the cat. It was a picture of Ellie's painting that she had taken on her phone and then had printed out on the university's large format printer.

"So you've had another thought about where this is?" she asked.

Kathryn looked up from her prone position. "Yes. I think I've been considering the wrong Aldborough. Cazza's base was at Stanwick, near Richmond. There's a small place nearby called Aldbrough St. John. Slightly different spelling."

Putting the picture down on the coffee table, Den picked up Kathryn's iPad and opened Google Maps. It only took a few moments to find it.

"Why would she want to be buried there? It's in the middle of fucking nowhere, literally."

"Language, Den!" Kathryn exclaimed, covering Misty's ears with her hands.

Den snorted. "Lesbian stereotype, I told you." She clicked through some of the photos at the bottom of the screen—well-tended gardens, beautifully kept hedges, picture-perfect old stone cottages. There was no "street view." Somewhere the Google tentacles hadn't reached.

"God, it looks like a location for *Midsomer Murders*. Can't imagine the locals will want a media circus camped out on their pristine village green."

Kathryn picked Misty up and sat down in her recliner. "It's not far away. I think we should take a look. See if it bears any resemblance to Ellie's painting." The kitten made herself at home on Kathryn's lap and started to purr. They both looked content.

"Sure." Den tried to rein in her feelings. It was too stupid to be jealous of a cat. "Do you think we should ask Ellie to come along? Her intuition could be useful. Like that woman who was convinced Richard III's bones were lying under the car park."

"You don't really believe Ellie is *communicating* with Cartimandua?"

"Rob seems to think so."

155

"They've both spent too much time on that hill. Are you sure they don't indulge in smoking weed?"

"I'm certain Ellie doesn't. Rob might. And Jo definitely does."

"She better clean up her act if she's going out with a cop." Kathryn was gently caressing the top of Misty's head.

"It didn't sound like the relationship was too advanced, Kat."

"You know, Den, I don't really like being called Kat."

"You've never told me not to."

"No. Well, for some reason I don't mind it from you."

Den smiled. "I do count for something, then."

Kathryn stopped stroking the kitten and reached across the space between them. "You know you do."

Den took her hand and held on. "Anyway, you're avoiding the subject. Do we ask Ellie to come along to Aldbrough St John with us? Or should we just do a quick inspection on our own?"

"I think we should go on our own. If it looks like a possibility, then we can let her know."

"What about Misty?"

"What about her?"

"Will she be coming with us?"

Kathryn looked down at the dozing cat. "Maybe not this time. I guess she'll have to get used to being on her own sometimes."

"And what about sleeping arrangements?"

"I'm not sure she'll take to that basket. Cats aren't like dogs."

"So, she's sleeping with us?" Den had the feeling this had been decided already. Kathryn nodded and gave her the lopsided smile that always melted her insides

Den sighed. "Okay. But if she wees on me, she's out."

"Agreed." Misty had settled herself on Kathryn's chest, nestled comfortably between her breasts.

Den thought she and the kitten needed to have a serious chat before long about boundaries and which parts of the professor were off limits.

Jen Silver

Part Three

Answers

Chapter Seven

Robin stirred uneasily, aware of Ellie's wakefulness beside her. She didn't need to raise her eyelids far to know it was still dark outside.

"What's up, hon?" she asked, rolling onto her back.

Ellie didn't answer right away. She snuggled up close and Robin could feel the dampness of her skin. It was cold in the room and Ellie was well past the menopausal stage, so there had to be another reason.

"You're all clammy," she said, moving her arm so she could properly embrace the smaller woman. "Bad dream?"

"Not really. Just intense. I'm trying to hold onto the details. They're important."

Robin waited, resisting the temptation to caress the breasts that were now pressed into her side. She was aroused by Ellie's closeness, clammy or not.

"El? Are you okay?" she asked gently after a few more minutes of silence.

"Mm. When we were in London, the night after the exhibition I had this dream. It was when Cartimandua first started to communicate with me. That was when she said they wanted to go home."

Robin sighed. She reached over to switch on the bedside lamp and waited for Ellie to continue.

"I know you find this hard to believe, sweetie, but it's true. And just before I woke up this morning, she spoke to me again. Her treasure is resting in a secure place here. Vellocatus says it's hidden inside the granary, five paces west from the rear wall, that's the north end."

"And where is this granary? The dig didn't turn up anything like that."

"I don't know. She didn't say."

"How tall was Vellocatus? I mean, say we do find out where this granary was, how big were her paces?"

"I think she was about your height. We would have to know her shoe size. Ed could tell us that." Ellie moved away from her and propped herself up on one elbow. Her blue eyes held Robin's in a steady gaze. "I know this is hard for you, Rob, but your support means everything to me."

"You'll always have that, my love. It doesn't matter what anyone else thinks." Robin pushed a stray hair back from Ellie's face. "We'll have our very own adventure. The Famous Five go to Starling Hill."

"You do believe then…that there's buried treasure here?"

"Eighteen months ago we didn't know there were royal remains here, let alone anything else. I believe we should at least take a look."

Ellie threw her arms around her. "You're the best."

"The best what?" Robin growled in her ear.

"The best…oh!" Ellie gasped as Robin's hand found its way between her thighs. "We don't have time for this. Our visitors will be arriving soon."

"It's early yet. And knowing Jas's navigation skills, they're sure to get lost." Robin kissed her, delighting in the wetness her fingers encountered in their exploration.

†

Jo had wakened to the sounds of energetic lovemaking in the next room. She checked the time on her phone. It was only six, a bit early for her hosts' regular morning exercise. Harry looked up from his prone position next to her.

"I think a pre-breakfast walk is in order, don't you?"

As "walk" was his second favorite word, after "food," he immediately got off the bed and stretched. Jo followed more slowly. She dressed quietly and tiptoed down the stairs to use the loo there so as not to disturb Ellie and Robin.

She set up the coffee maker before going out. A heavy frost lay everywhere and the cloudless sky indicated it would

161

be a bright but cold day. Harry ran on ahead of her, stopping only to pee on the gatepost before entering the field.

It would be a few hours before the next two visitors from London arrived. Henry and Paul had been easy to be with, and Paul's almost childlike delight in everything he saw had been charming. Jo wasn't sure the return of Jasmine Pepper to the farm would be such a lighthearted experience. Jo remembered that Jasmine had been a rather sullen presence during her visit the summer before. But she was bringing her new girlfriend, so maybe she had mellowed.

Anyway Jo's main task today was to keep busy and try not to think too much about the dinner date with Ash. The first pottery class was on Thursday, and no matter how often Ellie told her it would be fine, she couldn't help feeling nervous. Today she would go over everything again to make sure she hadn't missed any steps.

Her feet moved automatically along the sheep trodden trail. Harry came back to her with a stick he'd found. She threw it for him and he bounded off in pursuit. Looking around she realized they'd wandered a long way from the farm and were now on Owen Chappell's land. Jo called to Harry, anxious to head back. The farmer wouldn't hesitate to shoot either of them if he caught them trespassing. Although he had apologized for having shot Denise when she'd inadvertently strayed into one of his fields in her misguided attempt to find a cross-country route to Starling Hill while the dig was on.

Reaching the farmyard at last, Jo's stomach rumbled, reminding her that breakfast would be a good idea. Robin was standing by the chicken run with what looked like a full basket of eggs.

"Morning," she called.

Robin turned to face her. "You're out early."

"Yeah, well, we had a pre-dawn wake up call."

"Oh?"

Jo watched Robin's expression change to one of embarrassment.

"Um, sorry about that. We were both awake, so…"

"Don't apologize. It's your house. Anyway, what's so fascinating about the chickens this morning." The hens were pecking the ground obsessively in their search for any loose grain.

"Just thinking." She shook her head. "Yeah, I know, that's dangerous. Especially before breakfast. Come on, I'm starving."

Harry was waiting for them by the door and dashed in ahead when Robin opened it.

"I guess someone else wants their breakfast now."

Jo laughed. The smell of coffee reached them and her tummy made its presence known again. "Me too."

†

The last time she'd driven here, Jasmine had thought she was on her way to spend an idyllic week with Robin, not knowing what she would find at the farm. Steph was driving this time, and when they reached the Huddersfield ring road, Jas knew she needed to concentrate on finding the right turn.

"You sure you're okay with this?" Steph asked.

"Yes." Jas glanced at Steph's profile, her lover's knuckles showed white as she gripped the steering wheel tightly. Placing a reassuring hand on her thigh, she said, "We've been over this, babe. I'm all yours."

"Hm." Steph kept her eyes fixed on the road.

"Anyway, we're not staying long. And Robin might not even be there."

"Shit. Wasn't that the turn off?"

Jas hadn't been watching and realized too late that they had passed the exit for the road leading to Starling Hill. *Welcome to ring road hell*, she thought, as they passed the university buildings.

"Come on, Jas. You've been here before."

"Only once. And circled the town three times before I got it right."

†

Ellie paced around her work area. She wasn't going to get much done with their visitors arriving soon. Robin had gone off with the shopping list since it looked like they would need to provide lunch for Jasmine and Steph.

The queen was quiet today. Probably resting after making her presence known in Ellie's dreams. Ed hadn't questioned why she wanted to know Vee's shoe size; he just texted back that he thought eight would be right. Robin was seven or seven and a half, depending on the make.

The next problem was how to find the granary. Ellie located one of the aerial photos Kathryn had obtained when she was gathering evidence that Starling Hill was a possible Roman site. If the granary were an Iron Age structure, then it would likely have been made of wood and there would now be no trace. But if it had been constructed after the queen moved here, then they might have used stone, having learned from the Romans.

✝

"Is all this land theirs?" Steph asked as she negotiated the rutted track up to the farm.

"Yes." Jas was glad they had arrived on a sunny day. The bare moorland in the distance almost looked inviting. She was surprised to see that the farmyard looked much the same as it had when she last saw it. Even the camper van was still there.

"You can park behind the Corsa. As far as I know it's just scrap metal." Jas waited for Steph to open her door. They played this game because they both enjoyed it. Jas anticipated her lover's touch as she held out a hand to help her down. Steph's strong arm steadied her and she leaned into the warm embrace. The smile on Steph's face told her there would be some action as soon as they were on their own.

Their first welcome at the farm came from the black and white dog bounding up to greet them.

"Harry," a voice called. "Sorry, he has no manners."

Jas recognized the woman who appeared from the direction of the barn. This was Jo Flashy Knickers, or some such stupid name, Jas recalled. She was saved from having to say anything as Jo introduced herself to Steph first.

"Hi, I'm Jo. You must be Stephanie."

"Just Steph, thanks."

"Good timing. Lunch is ready. Would you like to freshen up first?"

As that was a polite euphemism for using the toilet, Jas spoke up. "Yes, that would be nice. Thanks." She decided to aim for the cheerful end of the spectrum, as she was sure she hadn't made a great impression on her previous visit.

Jo led the way into the house. Jas remembered how dark it had seemed inside even in summer. Maybe it was the familiarity, as well as Steph's comforting presence by her side, but it looked more welcoming now. The tabby cat, the smaller of the two, was stretched out in the living room armchair. She suspected the large ginger cat was in the kitchen where the food was. He'd always seemed to be lurking there.

Jasmine slipped into the downstairs bathroom while the other two carried on into the kitchen. She heard Ellie's voice welcoming Steph before she closed the door. This time Jas had dressed more appropriately for a visit to the farm but she still wasn't willing to totally relinquish style over comfort in her attire. She realized that her colorful Aztec print leggings, which didn't look out of place on Oxford Street, were more like something Jo Whatsit would wear here. The plain black cashmere sweater was classy though. She took one more glance in the mirror to check her hair, and then ventured out to see what Ellie was serving for lunch. Whatever it was, she hoped there was a glass of wine or beer to go with it.

†

Stepping into the farm's kitchen, Steph thought she had gone back in time. The Aga stove taking up one wall could have come straight out of a Joanna Trollope novel. The decorative flagstones covering the floor and a sturdy wooden table made the room appear to be only missing the presence of a few large and slobbering dogs. She supposed the border collie that had greeted them filled that role. The ginger cat on the window ledge could have been a set prop as well.

"How was the drive?" Ellie was asking.

Steph gave herself a mental shake and turned her attention to the small blonde standing by the table. "Not bad, thanks. It was a steady run. We didn't hit any major holdups."

"Oh, good. Well, everything's ready. Please have a seat. What would you like to drink?"

"A beer, if you've got one."

"Of course. Do you know what Jasmine would like?"

"Probably the same."

The woman, who had introduced herself as Jo, opened the fridge and took out four bottles of Corona. Turning to Ellie she asked, "White wine?"

"Please."

Jas arrived in the kitchen just as Steph took the first sip from her bottle. Ellie greeted her with the distant politeness she had already observed between her lover and Jo.

"Something smells good," she said, in an effort to warm up the atmosphere.

"Yes, I've made a tomato and lentil soup. I hope that's acceptable for everyone."

"Lovely."

"Jo, would you get the bread out of the oven, while I serve the soup? And do you know where Robin is?"

"Sure. She was pacing around the field. I called out to her and she waved. I guess she knows lunch is ready."

"I'll leave hers in the pot. She can help herself when she comes in." Ellie ladled soup into bowls. As Jo handed them out, Steph noticed each one had a different pattern.

"Did you make these?" she asked as Ellie sat down.

"Yes. All our mugs, plates, bowls, and serving dishes were made here. Usually I keep the rejects. If you look at that one closely, the pattern didn't take properly on one side."

"Did you make the bread as well?"

"No. I wish I had the time. We stockpile it in the freezer; however, it smells and tastes like the real thing when heated up."

The only sounds that could be heard for the next few minutes were ones of appreciation as they ate their soup. Steph picked up a piece of bread and wondered if it would be considered bad form to dip it in the soup. Ellie caught her eye and nodded.

"We don't stand on ceremony here. That bread is made for dipping."

Steph smiled and dipped. Whatever frostiness existed between Jas and the other two women didn't seem to extend to her.

"What's Robin looking for? Has she lost something?" Jas had finally looked up from her bowl.

Jo and Ellie exchanged looks before the farm owner answered. "Just doing a bit of research. It may not amount to anything."

Before Steph had time to wonder what was really going on, Robin burst in, followed closely by Harry. The dog went over to his owner and put his head on her knee. Jo patted his head, saying softly, "You don't like lentils."

Robin grabbed the bottle of beer Jo had left for her at the place setting next to Ellie and took a long swig. Steph felt a surge of the jealousy that had gripped her when they met in London. The red-haired woman's vitality and overt sexiness was palpable. And it didn't escape her observation that Robin had slept with the other three women at the table.

"Hey, hon." Ellie reached over and tugged on her belt loop to pull her lover close. "Sit down and I'll get you some soup."

"I'm good. I'll just drink this. So, Steph, your rust bucket made it up here."

"Yes, no problem. Henry didn't seem keen to lend me his car."

"Not surprised. He thought the stone walls were a menace, out to get him." Robin finished her beer. She looked at Ellie who had got up and ladled soup into a mug. "I need to show you something."

"Fine. And you need to have this."

Robin took the mug from her, kissed the top of her head. "Excuse us," she said as she pulled Ellie out of the room.

†

Jas waited until they heard the outer door close before turning her gaze on Jo.

"What's going on? They're acting weird, even for them."

Jo looked down at Harry who was still gazing at her with an "I might like lentils now" look in his eyes.

"Come on, Jo."

"I really can't say. You'll have to ask them."

Soames had roused himself from his window ledge and was sniffing at the pot of soup Ellie had left on the counter. Deciding it wasn't to his taste, he jumped down and wandered out of the room tail held high. Jo would have liked to get up and follow him.

Jas was still looking at her intently. "Is this because of last year? Look, I know I behaved badly then, but it's all water under the bridge now. A lot of things have changed. I've changed."

Steph intervened before Jo could think of a response. "Babe, you're putting Jo on the spot. She's right. We can talk to Ellie and Robin. And it may be none of our business anyway."

Jo smiled at her. Meeting Steph in the yard earlier, she had been surprised by her appearance, a polar opposite to the always immaculately turned out Jasmine. So maybe Jas had changed, but the mistrust was still there.

"Come on, Jas. You can show me the field, and then we'll head up to Durham."

"I'd be happy to give you a tour of the pottery studio as well." Jo didn't want Steph to leave feeling she hadn't been made welcome at the farm.

"That would be great, thanks."

"Okay. I'll just wash these up and join you outside."

"Can we help?"

"No. It won't take long and I know where everything goes."

"Well, if you're sure."

Jo watched them leave with a sigh of relief, pleased that Steph had forestalled any further interrogation. She washed the dishes and put the bottles in the recycling bin by the door. Unable to ignore Harry's pleading looks any longer, she gave him one of the doggy treats kept in a container on top of the fridge.

†

Den planned to get an article drafted before their visitors arrived. The morning had started well with fifteen hundred words and only a few quotes needed to fit in. She was happy with the overall shape and tone. A bit more polishing and it would be ready to send off.

Misty had left her alone while she was writing but now seemed at a loose end. When Den stopped her from clawing at the sofa, the kitten nipped her finger and gave her arm a playful tap with a tiny paw.

"You want to play, huh?"

Den found the ball of string Kathryn had been teasing the creature with the night before. While she was lying on the floor trying to replicate the previous evening's activity, she saw the tattered remnants of a glove by the chair. On closer inspection she realized it was one of the professor's digging gloves. This explained why Misty had left her in peace all morning.

The kitten was now chasing a moving shard of sunlight, trying to place its paws on the bright spot as the shifting clouds created a dancing pattern across the carpet. Den laughed as she picked her up.

"Mummy's not going to be pleased with you. Let's see what else you've been doing today."

The bedroom looked to be disaster free at first glance. Den had tidied up after Kathryn left for work, placing their hastily discarded underwear in the laundry basket. However, Misty had managed to pry the closet door open and spread sandals and shoes around, some of them now displaying small teeth marks. Finding them too tough, she had opted for the glove and taken her prize into the living room.

"Thanks, bud. Now I'll be in trouble for not closing the door properly." A small yawn greeted this remark.

Still carrying the kitten, Den headed into the kitchen. Time for another cup of coffee and a sandwich before she needed to think about preparing for Jas and Steph's arrival. There wasn't much to do apart from clearing up Misty's trail of destruction. Jas had insisted they would stay at a B&B, so Den just needed to stock up on wine and beer and a few nibbles, giving them something restorative after their long drive before going out for dinner.

Placing Misty in her basket, Den turned her thoughts to how she was going to entertain the two Londoners for the next few days. Durham's sights could easily be covered in a morning. Kathryn had offered the use of her car, so depending on the weather, Den could take them to the coast. It was a half hour drive to Seaham. Not much there but it was known as the Durham Heritage Coast and was a Site of Special Scientific Interest with a variety of birdlife. She didn't think it would be of much interest to Jas, but Steph was more of an outdoors type. Den just hoped Jas had packed sensible footwear.

Thursday afternoon was the day she and Kathryn were planning to visit Aldbrough St John. So that could be another trip out for their visitors. The professor could probably be persuaded to give them a tour of the Roman fort site at Binchester as well.

†

"This had better be good, Rob. Whatever will they think of us? Drove all this way and you can't even be bothered to sit down with them for lunch."

Robin didn't answer. She kept walking and Ellie had to trot to keep up. When they reached the back of the chicken coop, her lover stopped abruptly and Ellie bumped into her. Robin pointed, using the hand holding the mug, tomato and lentil soup threatening to slop over the sides.

"This is it!"

"What do you mean? It's a pile of rocks."

"Don't you see? The granary was probably separate from the main part of the settlement. That's why it's not in the field."

Ellie caught on. "And grain was a precious commodity. It would have needed a dry and secure storage area."

"How long have these stones been here?"

"Forever and a day. Dad was planning to use them to teach me how to build a dry stone wall."

174

Robin, knowing how much Ellie had loved her father, wrapped a comforting arm around her shoulders. "Too bad he didn't. We'll have to shift these ourselves."

"But it might not be under here. It could be in the coop or in the pen."

The squat stone building had always been used as a chicken coop in Ellie's memory. The thick walls provided an impenetrable barrier for predators.

"Well, I think we should start here before we think about disturbing Minerva and Luna, and the rest."

Ellie smiled. Robin never could remember the names for the chickens, all Roman goddesses.

"Okay. But before we start, you're going to eat your soup."

"It's too thick to drink," Robin protested.

"I'll get you a spoon."

†

The field had an unfamiliar manicured look, the smooth turf of a football pitch. In Jasmine's memory, it was covered in sparse, much chewed over, sheep-trodden grass with the occasional clump of wildflowers making an appearance.

"It looks so different," she said to Jo, who joined them as they stood gazing out at the terrain.

"The university returfed it once the dig was finished."

"They made a good job of it," Steph commented.

"You can go in and walk around, if you want," Jo offered. "There's only that bit of Roman-built wall left exposed." She pointed to the short row of stones near the top of the field. "We use it as a bench now."

Harry wriggled past them through a gap between the gate and the hedge. He went straight to a spot halfway down the field and pawed at the grass, sniffing all around.

"That's where he found the first bone. He's never forgotten it. I don't think he's ever forgiven me for not letting him keep it." Jo opened the gate.

Jas hung back and let Jo go ahead with Steph. *Had it been a mistake to come back here?* Seeing Robin in London hadn't been a problem. But here was another matter. Robin's disheveled appearance, exuding raw energy when she came into the farmhouse kitchen, had sent an unexpected jolt of desire straight to her clit. Memories of the times they had fucked pulsed through her body.

When she told Jo she had changed, it was true. And she loved Steph. What they had together was special. Robin had only ever been part of a series of one-night stands. Jas dragged her mind, and her treacherous body, back to the present. Jo was showing Steph where the skeletons had been found and explaining in detail how the bones had been carefully uncovered. The gardener looked like she was interested, asking questions. Jas took in a few deep breaths before joining them.

Steph turned to her. "This is amazing, isn't it, babe? You wouldn't believe they could have been here so long without anyone knowing. But seeing this place, I can understand it better."

"Yes." Jas couldn't trust herself to say anything else. She slipped an arm around her lover's waist, just wanting to reconnect with her solid presence.

"Well, it's a bit nippy out here. The wind's getting up." Jo beamed at them. "Shall we go and have a look at the studio?"

Jas had to admit to being surprised by Jo's hosting skills. She'd thought she was a real flake when she'd first met her. All the junk she made out of recycled crap and sold on a market stall. Now she was acting like she owned the place.

The studio had changed as well. The first room was clearly an artist's space but neatly kept. Ellie's anal tendencies, Jas suspected.

Steph stopped in front of the easel and looked at the painting in progress. "Where's this?" she asked.

"I don't know." Jo looked a bit uncomfortable. "Ellie often paints scenes from memory. The pottery studio's in here."

Jas had the same feeling she'd had earlier in the kitchen. *They were hiding something, this lot,* she thought, as they obediently followed Jo into the next room. The setup here was as she'd remembered from her first visit, standing in the doorway, seeing Robin who didn't look thrilled to see her. She only half listened as Jo talked Steph through the process, showing her the raw clay, the wheel, the kiln, a row of plates waiting to be glazed.

When they finally emerged from the barn, Jas was relieved to hear Steph say, "Thanks for the tour, Jo. It's been great, but I think we'll need to set off now."

"Yes, of course."

"I'd like to thank Ellie for lunch. Do you know where she is?"

"Um, I guess the only other place she could be if she's not in the house, is with the chickens."

"Oh, and we haven't seen them. Paul said we should see the chickens."

Jas bit her tongue. She didn't want to spoil the day for Steph, but the farm was really bringing out her inner bitch.

They walked across the yard to satisfy Steph's desire to look at some scrawny hens pecking around. As they neared the enclosure they could hear voices.

"That sounds like Ellie. Come on, Jas, we'll just say goodbye." Steph seemed to have finally picked up on her mood.

The sight that greeted them as they rounded the end of the small building wasn't something Jas could have predicted. Robin was sitting on a pile of stones, spooning soup out of a mug. Ellie was standing a few feet away pointing at something on the ground. They both looked shifty when they realized they had company, but Ellie recovered herself quickly.

"Oh, I'm so sorry. We haven't been very good hosts."

"That's okay. Jo's given us the grand tour. Just wanted to say thanks for a lovely lunch. We'll be on our way now." Steph was at her diplomatic best.

"Well, it's been wonderful to see you both. You'll have to stay longer next time."

Not if I can help it. Jas managed a weak smile as Ellie gave them each a brief hug. Robin just waved her spoon.

She gave a mental sigh of relief when they were finally settled in the van and headed down the lane.

†

"Thanks, Jo. You're a hero. Do you think they suspected anything?" Robin had put her mug down and was starting to move the stones as the sound of the van rattling down the lane receded.

"They'd have to be thick as those stones if they didn't. What's so important that you couldn't even join us for lunch?" Jo glanced between Ellie and Robin.

"We think this might be where the coins are hidden." Ellie added a stone to the pile Robin had started.

"Really." Jo looked at the undiminished pile of hefty rocks. "In that case, you should have invited them to stay. I'm sure Steph could have given you a hand shifting this lot."

"Naw. The less they know, the better." Robin grunted as she tried to move one of the larger stones.

"Well, Den and Kathryn will probably fill them in, so it's not going to be much of a secret for long."

"Anyway, Jo, feel free to pitch in."

"Sorry. I've got market stuff to sort out for tomorrow, and then a dinner date to prepare for."

"Oh yeah, the hot cop."

"Don't call her that." Jo could feel herself blushing.

"Why not? She's hot for you and she's a cop."

"Rob, leave off." Ellie came to Jo's rescue. "If you're looking for something to wear tonight, Sophie left some clothes here. I'm sure she wouldn't mind."

"Thanks. I was going to ask." Jo had noticed the clothes in the closet that obviously didn't belong to either Robin or Ellie. She had her eye on a silk blouse that looked like it would fit. Ellie's son's partner was definitely more in tune with today's fashions than Jo could ever be.

She left them to their work and went to her van. After checking her supplies for the next day at the market, she would have a nice long bath and give in to more thoughts of Ash. *Hot cop, indeed.*

†

Afternoon traffic was building up on the motorway as they approached the Leeds junction.

"It should ease up once we get past the city," Jas said.

These were the first words Jasmine had uttered since they left the farm. P!nk was just hitting her stride on "Bad Influence" when Steph reached over to turn the volume down.

"You're still hot for her, aren't you, babe?"

"Not really." Jas was staring out the window, her face hidden from view by a curtain of hair, but her hands gave her away, clenched in her lap. "Being there, it just brought back memories."

"Was she that good? I knew I should have decked her when I had the chance."

Jas looked at her now and Steph wanted to reach over and brush away the tears visibly streaming down her lover's face.

"I'm sorry. I guess it wasn't a good idea to go there," she said, swiping at her eyes.

"Well, the inhabitants hardly seem to be members of your fan club." Steph decided to try for a lighter tone.

"Jo's all right, once you get past the trippy-hippy thing."

Steph agreed. She also thought Ellie was a genuinely nice person. Her frostiness towards Jas was understandable given the past history with Robin. She kept her eyes on the road, wishing the miles away. All she wanted to do was take Jas in her arms and show her how much she was loved. And that's what she intended to do as soon as they were booked into their room at the bed and breakfast in Durham.

†

Pacing back and forth in her living room, Ash wondered how she would make it through the evening

181

without making an idiot of herself. Jo deserved better than what she could offer, if her experience with Shona Gibson was anything to go by.

Jo had insisted on driving over in her van, even though Ash offered to pick her up. The brightly colored camper van rattled into her driveway just as she was giving in to the thought that this was all a big mistake. She should have just left herself with the memory of a pleasant dinner date the week before. That idea went up in smoke when she opened the door to find Jo smiling at her, brown eyes sparkling, as she held out a bottle of wine.

"Thanks. You didn't need to bring anything." *Just yourself,* she wanted to add, but decided it sounded too creepy. "Come on in."

Ash took Jo's jacket, hung it up on the rack by the door, and led the way into her living room.

"Wow, great view," Jo said.

"Yes. It was the main reason for buying the house, as well as the decent sized garden at the back. That's why I said you could bring Harry."

"Sweet of you, but Robin offered to look after him for the evening."

"Okay. What would you like to drink?"

"A glass of red would be good, thanks."

"Right. Have a seat. I'll be back in a tick." Ash went into the kitchen. If either Robin or Ellie had helped Jo decide what to wear, they had chosen well. The filmy gray silk blouse and black chinos didn't look like items of clothing that would be found in Jo's wardrobe.

Ash poured out the wine and checked on the casserole. It was simmering away nicely. As long as her guest didn't look in her bin, she wouldn't know it was from Marks & Spencer. The addition of a few more veggies and a splash or two of wine would, she hoped, give it a more homemade look.

Jo wasn't sitting down when she returned with the wine glasses. The other woman seemed entranced by the fireplace. Ash glanced around in a momentary panic. Had she removed the photo that normally had pride of place on the mantle?

"Nice stone work," Jo said, turning to look at her.

"Thanks. I did it myself."

"Gosh. That's amazing."

"I like to keep busy when I'm not working."

"So, have you been cooking all day, as well? Smells great."

It occurred to Ash that Jo was possibly as nervous as she was. Her most recent relationship hadn't ended well either from what she'd said about the woman on the boat. Avoiding the question about her cooking skills, Ash motioned for Jo to join her on the sofa, handing her the glass of wine after they sat down.

"What have you been doing today? More pottery?" Ash asked. Might as well get Jo to talk, as she wasn't ready to do much talking herself.

†

The food was lovely but Jo suspected it had come from a supermarket ready meal. However, Ash had gone all out on the table setting with fresh flowers and candles. The dining room windows looked onto the back garden. It was too dark to really see anything, but as there were no neighboring houses in view, Ash left the curtains open and they sat there long enough to see the moon appear over the tops of the trees.

Their conversation over dinner had skated over general topics, and Ash entertained her with stories about the people she met in her job, but Jo had the feeling there was something she wanted to tell her. When they moved into the living room and were seated with their coffee, she decided to try to find out.

"This is a big house for just one person. I thought you might have a dog, or at least a cat or two. Must get lonely at times."

The silence that followed this comment seemed to stretch out forever. Ash looked away from her, into the fireplace, which now held brightly burning coals.

The pain in Ash's blue eyes when she turned to face her made Jo wish she could take the words back. "I'm sorry."

"I really like you, Jo. But I haven't been able to form any kind of relationship since Cos, my last girlfriend. I just seem to shut down as soon as it looks like sex might be involved." Ash was staring at the carpet between her knees.

Jo tentatively reached over and started to rub her back gently. "I like you too, Ash. Right now I'm happy with whatever you can offer."

"What if I don't have anything to offer?"

"I think you do. And I don't mind waiting."

"You could be waiting a long time."

"I'm guessing Cos must have been in the photograph that was on the mantelpiece."

Ash looked up at her, eyes wide. "How do you know that?"

"Doesn't take an ace detective. The frame-shaped dust-free space is a giveaway."

"Oh great. Now you know I'm a lousy housekeeper as well."

The desire to trace her fingers across the blonde fuzz on Ash's head was almost too strong to resist, but Jo knew it wasn't the right time. She stopped her impromptu back rub and said, "Why don't you tell me about her?"

After a few heavy sighs, Ash said, "Okay. Why not?" She sat up straighter and Jo thought for a moment she was going to whip out her police notebook. Then she began to speak, softly at first, gaining in confidence as Jo listened patiently.

"We joined up at the same time and went through training together. I was only eighteen and although I knew I was gay, I didn't know if she was. And I was too shy to ask. When we graduated we were assigned to different divisions. When our paths crossed again, six years later, she was a qualified dog handler. By the end of that year we'd moved in together. Clarissa Cosgrove. Like me, she didn't want to be called by her first name. She was always Cos." Ash got up and walked over to the rolltop desk in the corner. She came back to hand Jo a framed photo.

Jo saw two smiling women with a serious looking German Shepherd between them. Ash's hair was shoulder length. The other woman had wavy dark brown hair that fell over her eyes, an open face. The kind of person you would immediately take to if you met her at a party.

"Cos and Ben. He was two when the photo was taken. She'd had him for three years the day she died."

"She died. Oh my God, Ash."

Ash stood by the window, looking out at the darkness. "I wasn't on shift that day. When two cops showed up at the door, even though they were friends and not in uniform, I knew. I've delivered enough death messages in my time. Cos had been on a fairly routine job chasing down a robber. Ben flushed him out of his hiding place. Unfortunately, no one knew the perp was armed. He shot Cos in the head. Not really a good move. Ben went for him, latched onto his arm as trained and sat on his chest. The guy couldn't move until other officers arrived on the scene. Another dog handler got Ben to move, but then he went and lay down next to Cos. They had to tranquilize him to be able to get her into the ambulance. Not that it was any use. She was gone by then."

"When did this happen?"

"Five years ago. We had just bought this house but hadn't actually moved in. The garden would have been ideal for Ben. He was a lovely dog, as long as he wasn't on duty. We had to find a place away from a main road since he would get excited if he heard sirens. I wanted to keep him but he was immediately assigned to another handler. I guess Cos would have wanted that for him. She wouldn't have wanted his training to go to waste."

She wouldn't have wanted you to go to waste, either. Jo looked down at the photo again, her eyes pricking with tears. Ash was still standing by the window. Jo put the photo down carefully on the sofa and went to her. When she put her arms around her, Ash stiffened. "I just want to hold you. It's okay. I'm not asking for anything more." *Yet.*

Chapter Eight

The tip of a tongue tickled her cheek and Kathryn smiled. She reached out to let Den know she was awake but there was only empty space. A small paw landed on her face and she realized it was Misty giving her a wakeup call, not her lover.

Catching hold of the kitten, she struggled to sit up with the small creature wriggling in her grasp. "Hasn't Den fed you?"

The loud meow indicated her words were understood. Kathryn had always thought people who talked to their pets like they were humans were certifiable. Now she was going to have to put herself in that category.

"Just let me go to the bathroom and we'll remedy the situation." *Certified nut-job, no doubt.*

Misty watched her pee and wash her face. Kathryn tied the belt on her robe and picked up the kitten. The smell of coffee brewing drew her into the kitchen. Den was sitting at the table typing on her laptop.

"Hey, I didn't want to wake you."

"Well, someone else did." Kathryn filled the kitten's food bowl and set it on the floor. She waited for Misty to settle down to eat before helping herself to coffee and joining Den at the table.

"Steph seems all right."

"Jas obviously thinks so." Den shut down her laptop and closed the lid.

"When are you setting off?"

At dinner the night before the two Londoners were thrilled with the idea of going to the seaside for the day.

"I'm picking them up at half nine. Gives them time to have a shag before breakfast."

"Really, Den!"

"You saw the way they were looking at each other. I thought they were going to go for it in the restaurant."

The paw on her leg let Kathryn know Misty wanted to be picked up. She lifted the kitten onto her lap and was rewarded with the sound of a contented purr.

"She's easily satisfied." Den finished her coffee and stood to fetch some more. She refilled both their mugs and kissed Kathryn lightly on the head. "I don't suppose you have time for us to…you know…before you go to work."

"No." She reached up and pulled Den's head down to give her a proper kiss. "I would like to, but there's a departmental meeting at nine."

Den sat back down. "Would it be okay to take Jas and Steph over to Binchester after they've dipped their toes in the North Sea?"

"Are they really interested in old ruins? They might find Beamish more interesting."

"Is it still open?"

"I think so. At least until the start of November." Kathryn watched Den process the idea. The open-air museum had a lot to offer. The living history of North East England in the last century was created with replica buildings, and actors in authentic period costumes playing shopkeepers, miners, and farmers.

"Yeah. They'd probably like that. I don't think they'll want to spend a lot of time on the beach. It's a bit breezy out there."

Kathryn stood and placed the kitten on Den's lap. "Well, whatever you end up doing, have a good day."

"Hey, what about Misty? She'll be home alone all day."

"I can pop back at dinner time to check on her." She caught Den's look of surprise and laughed. "Better get used to the terminology, love. You're in the North now. Dinner is lunch and supper is tea."

"Aren't you having any breakfast, or whatever it's called up here?"

"No. We'll be having pastries at our meeting. I better get a move on." Kathryn stroked the kitten and gave Den a quick kiss on the lips before heading back to the bedroom to get ready for work.

†

Jo took the longer route through the town. Although Robin had given the van's engine a thorough tune up, she didn't relish getting stuck on one of the cross country routes where there was no phone signal.

The evening and night spent with Ash had been sweet. Jo had drunk a fair bit of wine and the police officer wouldn't allow her to drive back to the farm. She thought, initially, that Ash would offer the use of the spare bedroom. She had been prepared, and hoped for, an invitation to stay the night and went out to her van to collect the bag she'd brought with a change of clothes for the next day.

When she returned to the house she asked where she would be sleeping. Ash led her upstairs and opened the door to what was obviously her own bedroom. The queen-sized bed took up most of the room. Apart from the brightly patterned duvet, the room had a Spartan look. A dormitory just used for sleeping.

"Are you sure?" Jo asked.

"If you think you can handle it, I would like you to hold me tonight."

"I haven't brought anything to sleep in." Jo didn't add that she didn't actually own any nightwear.

"That's okay."

Jo had used the bathroom first and snuggled under the duvet just wearing her cotton briefs. She listened to Ash brushing her teeth and expected her to return fully covered up in flannel pajamas. Ash switched off the light when she came back so it was a shock for Jo to discover it was a naked body that climbed into the bed and lay down beside her.

After a brief silence, Ash said quietly, "I want to kiss you."

That first kiss was something Jo thought she would never forget. Whatever happened between them, that kiss would linger in her memory for a long time. They kissed and cuddled like two teenagers, unsure of what to do next. It was all Jo could do to hold back. She knew she needed to let Ash set the pace, but it was hard to resist the temptation to go all the way. Her own juices were flowing freely and she desperately wanted Ash to touch her.

Before anything could happen, Ash let out a contented sigh, and within seconds she was asleep. Jo listened to her steady breathing and tried to get her own emotions under control. This was going to be the hardest thing she'd ever done, but she wanted this to work. She felt they had taken the first step towards liberating Ash from her self-imposed celibacy.

Ash was up before her in the morning and it was the smell of coffee wafting up the stairs that roused Jo from the deep sleep she'd fallen into after hours of wakefulness. Jo washed and dressed in the clothes she'd brought that were suitable for a day on the market stall. She found Ash in the kitchen, setting out breakfast supplies on the counter—marmalade, cereal, bananas. Two slices of bread were poking out of the toaster.

"Hey, sleepyhead. I didn't want to wake you." Ash smiled at her.

"The coffee did it. It's like a magnet."

They didn't talk about the night before over breakfast, but as she was getting ready to leave, Ash pulled her into a hug.

"Thank you for last night," she whispered.

Jo braked sharply as the vehicle in front came to a sudden stop. She swore at herself for daydreaming. These roadworks had been here for weeks, part of a lengthy gas pipeline replacement operation, so she should have been prepared. The collision of items in the back of the van brought forth more swearing. She could only hope none of the new pots had shattered.

†

The first sight of the sea brought exclamations of delight. Steph hoped Den wasn't thinking this whole trip had been a bad idea. Den's passengers had been behaving like a couple of kids on the drive over from Durham, pestering the driver with 'Are we there yet?' every few miles and singing along loudly to songs on the radio.

The exuberant mood was the result, Steph knew, of their lovemaking sessions. The door had barely closed on their arrival at the B&B when Jas grabbed her and pushed her forcefully onto the bed. This morning had been a bit more leisurely but still intensely satisfying. Steph was pleased she'd had the forethought to pack a few of their favorite sex toys.

Released from the car when Den parked, Steph and Jas ran towards the beach. The journalist caught up with them as Jas was removing her shoes.

"You'll freeze to death out here," Den warned.

"It feels wonderful. Come on, Steph."

Steph struggled to pull her trainers and socks off. Den was right, it was cold. But the sand did feel great between her toes.

When they tired of frolicking along the beach and finally started to feel the cold, Den drove them back inland where they found a welcoming pub and settled in for a cozy fireside lunch with beer.

Dinner the night before had been okay but it felt more like a formal occasion with the professor there. Kathryn had been perfectly pleasant to her even joking that they had something in common since they both liked digging in the dirt. Steph felt that was where any commonality ended. She had studied law at university, and knew she could hold her own on an intellectual level, but her lifestyle and Kathryn's were not likely to meet on any other plane.

Being with Den on her own was much more relaxing. Even though they had lived in the same house for several years, Steph was only recently getting to know her better. Jas was teasing the journalist, saying, "Now you've got a cat, the professor just needs to ditch the Civic for a Subaru."

Den didn't rise to the banter. She smiled enigmatically and sipped her pint of Black Sheep.

Steph commented on the drink. "I've bought this in bottles, but it tastes better from the tap."

"Yes, it does. Listen, I was thinking of taking you to Beamish. However, it's a bit nippy so, if you like real ale, how about going back to Durham, ditching the car, and embarking on a pub crawl?"

"Now that sounds like a plan! What do you think, babe?" Steph knew Jas wasn't a big beer drinker.

"Sure. You two can butch it up. I'll stick to white wine."

They were on their third pub when Jas brought up the topic of Starling Hill farm. Steph was surprised because she'd been warned off saying anything about their visit since Den was sensitive about Kathryn's infatuation with Ellie. Now though, after a gin and tonic and two large glasses of wine, Jas said, "There's something weird going down at the farm. Do you know what they're up to?"

"What do you mean, weird?" Den asked.

"Well, they were all looking a bit shifty. Even Jo, although she was acting quite normal compared to the other two, and that's saying something."

"When we left, Robin and Ellie were busy moving a pile of large stones from one place to another," Steph added.

Den looked around the room before lowering her voice. "Do you know about the burial plans?"

"The what? Who's died?"

"Well, there's still a lot of detail to work out, but the idea is that the bones of Queen Cartimandua and Vellocatus should be reinterred. Like they're going to do with Richard III. Only it wouldn't be in a church. In fact, Kat and I are going to look at a place tomorrow that we think might be the right location."

"But what has that got to do with the farm?" Jas's PR nose was on the scent.

"Yeah. If they're not being buried there, why were they shifting rocks?"

Den leaned further forward and whispered, "Buried treasure."

"You're shitting me. How strong is that beer?"

Sitting back, Den sighed. "I probably shouldn't have told you that."

"You're serious." Jas checked Den's expression.

"Anyway, I doubt whether they will find anything. The field was thoroughly excavated on Kathryn's dig."

Steph decided to pitch in. "But they weren't looking in the field. These rocks were behind the chicken house."

"Coop, babe. It's called a chicken coop." Jas smiled at her and Steph realized they were both well over their limit.

She glanced at Den. "Thanks for the tour today. We should go back to the B&B and sleep this off. We'll meet you later for dinner. Where are we going?"

Den gave her directions for the Italian restaurant she'd booked. "You can't miss it. It's right by the bridge."

†

Den watched them leave, Jas leaning on Steph as they stumbled out to the street. She reached for her phone and called Robin. It rang for a long time and Den was ready to end the call when it was finally answered.

"Hey mate, how's it going?" Robin sounded out of breath.

"Um, not good. I'm a little bit tipsy and I've just told Jas and Steph that you're looking for treasure."

Silence at the other end was followed by a big sigh. "Well, they would have found out sooner or later, I guess."

"So, have you found anything?"

"Not yet. We might know more once we've moved all these rocks. Ellie's trying to find an old plan of the farm. The building used as a chicken coop has been here as long as she remembers, but she did recall something her dad once said about it being part of a larger structure."

"I still don't get why you think it's a good idea to look there. Has she had instructions from the queen?"

"According to Vee, the hiding place was five paces west from the north end of the granary."

"So you think this building was the granary?"

"That's the idea."

"Well, sorry to disturb you."

"No worries. Glad of the break, this is hard work."

"Sorry to have let the cat out of the bag. Seems to be a habit of mine. Oh, yeah, speaking of cats…" Den filled Robin in on the arrival of Misty and Kathryn's obsession with her. "She's gone all broody on me."

Robin laughed. "Now that I would like to see."

Den ended the call and decided against another drink. She set off to walk along the river in an effort to sober up a bit before going back to the flat.

†

The day on the market passed more slowly than usual, and Jo's low mood was not improved by finding most of her previous week's pottery creations in bits. Cursing the lack of concentration that resulted in the emergency stop she'd had to make, she drank more coffee than she should and felt on edge all morning.

Trying to distract herself by thinking of the pottery class starting the next day didn't lift her spirits either. Despite Ellie's confidence that she could handle it on her own, Jo worried that she would freeze up completely and make stupid mistakes. She decided she would just have to ask Ellie to help her with the first session.

Her reverie was interrupted by a familiar voice. "Wow, these are way cool."

Jo looked up and shook the hair out of her eyes for a better view, not quite believing who she was seeing. "Tina?" The young woman staring back at her was indeed the university student she'd had a brief, but very sweet, fling with the year before.

"Yeah. Good to see you, Jo."

"You too. What are you doing here?"

"Came over to catch up with Jed. But he's not here." Tina had covered Jed's music stall for a few weeks the previous summer.

"No, he's in Skipton. I didn't know you still kept in touch."

"Oh, yeah. I help him keep up with new stuff on the scene."

"Right. Well, you're looking good." Jo wasn't sure about the bright blue hair coloring, but it was a fairly common sight in the town so Tina didn't look out of place. She was going to ask how her studies were going when a cyclist pulled up at the stall.

Ash grinned at Jo. "Can you take a break?"

"Um, yeah, I guess. I'll just ask Fergus…"

"I can look after it for a bit. It'll be just like old times." Tina was already ducking under the table to take her place.

"Okay. Thanks." Jo handed her the money pouch. "I won't be long."

"Take your time. I'll be fine." Tina looked at Ash. "I'll watch your bike if you want to leave it here."

Ash hesitated but then just nodded and wheeled it around behind the stall.

"Bit young for you, Jo. Or is she the long lost daughter you haven't mentioned?" Ash said as they walked across the road to the café.

"It's a long story."

"I mean, yeah, I can totally see you as a MILF."

Jo blushed at the abbreviation for "mother I'd like to fuck." She opened the door and ushered Ash inside before responding. "Tina had a crush on me last year. I was her first. Anyway she's got a girlfriend her own age now."

They ordered their coffees and sat down at the last available table near the counter.

Ash glanced down at the table, then looked up and reached for Jo's hand. "I'm sorry about last night. I really wanted to, you know."

"What are you sorry about?"

"I fell asleep on you, didn't I?"

Jo gazed into the concerned blue eyes. "I liked holding you. And, yes, I would like more. But, I'm not going to rush you. You set the pace. It's fine with me."

Ash let out a long breath. "I'll understand if you don't want to see me again."

"Ash, are you listening? I said, I can wait until you're ready."

"I might never be ready."

"I think you will. You'll know when the time is right."

"You're amazing, Jo."

"Not really. I've never lost anyone the way you have, but I have been left. And it hurts. I always say I'll never let it happen again, but then it does. Maybe I'm too trusting. I always want to believe in the best in people."

Ash's grip on her hand tightened. "I don't know why they left you, but I think they must have been nuts."

Fortunately their coffees arrived then. Jo was sure she would have kissed Ash at that moment otherwise.

Tina was just completing a sale of table mats made from recycled plastic bags when they arrived back at the stall. Jo smiled, recalling the time she'd shown Tina how to make them. Ash collected her bike and promised to come to the farm later.

Glancing at the tabletop, Jo noticed a few other items missing. "You've been busy," she said.

"Yeah. This stuff sells itself. I think you should get a shop."

"Sure, Tina. I can barely afford to keep myself and Harry."

"Anyway, she looks fit."

"Who?"

"You know who. The cyclist. You and her look good together."

"We're just friends."

"If you say so."

†

Robin stumbled into the kitchen drawn by the smell of toast and coffee. She ached all over and the simple act of getting out of bed had been tortuous. If this is what old age had in store for her, she would be making a trip to Switzerland.

Ellie glanced over, bemused, as she sat down slowly. "Can't take a bit of hard labor, hon?"

"Obviously not. I thought I was fitter than this. Why aren't you suffering?"

"Years of bending over a pottery wheel and keeping up with yoga exercises."

"Yoga's so boring."

"It's a state of mind." Ellie placed a mug of strong coffee in front of her. "Drink this. How many eggs do you want?"

"A double-yolker if we've got one."

"Coming right up."

Robin watched Ellie's easy movements as she cooked the eggs. It was a pity she'd been too knackered the night before to take advantage of Jo's absence to make love with Ellie in their favorite spot in front of the fire. She hoped the stiffness in her joints wore off soon.

Harry nosed her leg, looking up at her with his big brown eyes. "What's the matter buddy? You missing Jo?" Robin pulled on his ears and scratched the top of his head. "She'll be back later.

†

The rest of the day on the stall passed quickly. Tina stayed for another hour filling her in on her life. She'd had a summer job in a garden center and thoroughly enjoyed it, but still managed to have time off to go to the Leeds Festival.

"I looked for you there, Jo." They had gone to the outdoor music festival together the year before.

"No. I couldn't make it. Busy with other things." Things Jo didn't want to tell the youngster about, spoiling her sunny mood. She had been busy getting booted off the boat by Molly and having to find somewhere to live at short notice.

Tina fetched a sandwich for her before she left, taking the train into Manchester to meet up with other university friends.

Driving back to Starling Hill, Jo mused on the strangeness of the day. First waking up in Ash's bed, seeing Tina, then Ash. She hoped Ash would come to the farm as she'd promised, wondering if the police officer really did

203

want to get involved with her or if she was looking for an excuse to back off gracefully. It wasn't that Jo was engaged in any criminal activities, apart from occasionally smoking a little weed, but her way of life was on the fringe of normal society. Living at the farm for the last month was the closest to 'normal' she'd experienced for a while.

The farmyard seemed deserted when she pulled up, parking the van next to the Jeep. Harry appeared from behind the chicken coop as soon as she opened the door, leaping up for attention.

"Hey, I missed you too. And, no, I didn't forget your treat." She climbed down from the van and knelt so he could lick her face. After a quick cuddle, she stood and looked around. "So where is everyone?"

The dog set off towards the coop, looking back to see if she was following. Robin and Ellie were engaged in a close embrace when she rounded the corner of the building, standing on the bare patch of ground where the pile of stones had been.

Jo would have backed away discreetly, but Harry had no such inhibition, and nosed his way between the couple.

Robin looked up first and winked at her. "So, how was the hot cop?"

"Good."

"Only good? You did stay the night."

"Only because I'd had a fair bit to drink and she wouldn't let me drive home."

"You did sleep with her, though?"

"Yes. But we did only sleep."

Robin looked concerned. "Hey, if she's messing you about, I'll sort it."

"It's complicated."

"What's fucking complicated about it. She either wants to sleep with you or she doesn't."

Ellie joined in then. "Leave her alone, Rob."

Jo smiled to cover her embarrassment. "You two have been busy. I thought it would take longer to shift that lot."

"It would have if Robin hadn't been so determined to get to the bottom of it today. She'll be regretting it later." Ellie gave Robin's arm an affectionate squeeze.

"So what next?"

"We start digging."

"Yes. But not right now. Come on. I'm sure we could all do with a well-earned drink." Ellie moved out of Robin's embrace. "How was the market today, Jo?"

†

The evenings were getting colder and a chill wind was seeping through the windowpanes. Ellie left the bottle on the coffee table after she'd poured out three glasses of red wine. Robin finished lighting the fire and then settled on the floor between Ellie's legs to await the promised massage.

Jo told them about seeing Tina. "She's really come out of her shell."

"Must have been your good loving," Robin teased. Ellie pressed down hard on a knotted muscle making her lover yelp.

"Did she ever move back in with her parents?" Ellie asked, gently massaging Robin's sore areas. Tina had spent a few nights at the farm when her parents threw her out of the house late one night after discovering a stash of lesbian erotica in her bedroom.

"She made up with her mother, but has never really felt comfortable around her dad since. She's sharing a flat now with some other third-year students."

There was silence as they all sipped at their wine and stared at the flames leaping up the chimney. Ellie continued massaging Robin's shoulders and checked the whereabouts of the animals. Harry was curled up at Jo's feet, Soames was sleeping as close to the fire as he could without getting his fur singed, and she could feel Fleur's steady breathing as the cat lay draped across the back of her chair. Everyone accounted for, she could relax.

"Oh, and Ash came by while Tina was there. She's coming over this evening. You don't mind, do you?"

Ellie smiled at Jo. "Of course not. If she's here in time for dinner, there's plenty."

A groan from Robin. "Can you call her, Jo? Ask her to pick up a burger or two on her way through town."

"You like my vegetarian cottage pie!" Ellie pinched her playfully.

"Love it, hon. But Harry and I can't survive on vegetables alone."

"About Ash," Jo said hesitantly.

"What about Ash?" Robin looked up at her.

"Can I just ask that you lay off teasing about whether or not we're having sex? We're at a delicate stage. She might want to stay the night, but I'm not pushing her into it. Okay?"

"Okaaay." Robin drew the word out and Ellie knew without seeing her face that there was a big grin on it.

"Robin! Behave." Ellie saw Jo's anxious look. "Don't worry. We'll make her welcome."

†

Sitting at the kitchen table in the farmhouse, Ash was reminded of the first time she'd sat there after being called out in the middle of the night to check a possible disturbance. The only disturbing thing about that visit was sitting across from her now. On the ride home from the market, those deep brown eyes had stayed with her. The long hill climb up Cragg Vale had passed by without her noticing the change in altitude. After passing the reservoir at the top, Ash had pulled into a turnout to refocus, but she still needed a cold shower when she arrived home.

Ellie Winters telling her to help herself to gravy brought her back into the present. Ash tuned into the conversation.

"How do you know that's the place to dig?" Jo was asking Robin.

"Ellie says it feels right. Do you think I'd have spent two days of backbreaking labor if I didn't trust her intuition?"

Ash saw the sweet look that Ellie gave her partner and she felt her chest tighten. She and Cos had shared that kind of love. Could she really believe she would ever find that again?

"What are you digging up?" she asked.

Looks passed between the other three at the table. If she were in uniform she would have booked them for acting suspiciously.

Finally Robin said, "Might as well tell her. Den's already given the game away to Jas and Steph."

Ellie cleared her throat and gave Ash a brief smile. "There's a possibility that Cartimandua brought some of her wealth here. They didn't find much of value in the dig. Dr. Moss put this down to the fact that she probably had to leave her position in a hurry. However, the queen had been trading with the Romans for a long time. I believe, and I take full responsibility if nothing's found, that there is a considerable hoard buried here."

Ash looked around the table. They all seemed fairly sane. "You're not pulling my leg?"

"No. We're absolutely serious. But, as I say, it's only a possibility. That's why we were trying to limit the number of people who know about it. Now, I think that number is up to eight. If we do find anything we'll probably need to involve Ed. He's the head of the archaeology department at the university."

"Aren't there authorities you have to advise?"

"Yes. If we find anything, we'll contact PAS, the Portable Antiquities Scheme."

"Don't worry, officer. We will do everything by the book," Robin added.

After dinner, Ellie and Robin retired to their room, saying they were both ready for an early night. Ash helped Jo wash up, and then settled down with her on the sofa in the living room, to watch over the dying embers in the fireplace.

Jo snuggled up to her and the warmth of her body brought a feeling of peacefulness she hadn't experienced for a long time. Ash turned her head and was drawn into the intensity of Jo's eyes. She kissed her, tentatively at first, then with a mounting desire that overtook her previous inhibitions. The time had come. She was ready for the promise of love that Jo so freely offered.

When they paused for breath she said softly, "It's getting cold in here. Do you have a bed somewhere?"

Jo smiled and nodded. Without speaking she stood, took Ash's hand and led her up the stairs to her room. Harry followed but was told firmly to stay outside when they reached the door. He flopped to the floor with a resigned sigh and Jo gently closed the door on him.

Ash vaguely remembered removing clothes hastily before being overcome with the need not just to hold Jo but to give her the loving touch she had denied herself for so long.

†

Den's morning didn't quite go according to plan. Jas and Steph were occupying themselves looking around the town. They had agreed to meet at one o'clock when Kathryn returned from the uni and they could set off for Aldbrough St John.

The article she was writing took a back seat to searching the Internet for information on various coin hoards found in England. The Iron Age find at Honley in 1893 claimed to have contained a coin with Cartimandua's image on it. Other coins in that collection had the names of Volisius and Dumnocoverus, believed to be father and son. Volisius was also a contender for Cartimandua's father, but the connection was tenuous since he was of the Corieltauvi tribe based to the south and east of Brigantes territory.

Caught up in reading various reports of other Iron Age and Roman finds on British soil, Den didn't notice the hours slipping away. Misty also took up some of her time, demanding attention. Before she knew it, Jas and Steph were at the door and Kathryn was due back any minute.

Den closed her laptop on the unfinished article and berated the kitten. "It's your fault. Time waster."

†

Ash woke up in a strange room. Moving a hand tentatively she found only empty space beside her but the sheet was still warm. Memories of the night before flooded back and she smiled at the dust motes floating in the air above her head. The early morning sun was tracing a path across the low ceiling.

Jo came in, a dazzling vision dressed in a colorful sweater, carrying a misshaped mug.

"Coffee, as you like it."

Ash struggled to sit up clutching the sheet to her chest. "You're an angel."

Jo's smile brightened the room further. "I've never been called that." She sat down on the bed and put the mug on the bedside table.

"A coffee-bearing angel. And a sexy one, too." Ash brushed away a strand of hair. "Seems I'm always falling asleep on you."

"After your exertions last night, I'm not surprised."

"Was it good?" Ash couldn't keep the note of anxiety out of her voice.

"More than good. I would rejoin you in bed, but my first pottery students are arriving soon. The bathroom's all yours. Robin and Ellie are already up. And help yourself to whatever you want for breakfast."

"Okay."

Jo stood and Ash reached out to grasp her hand.

"Thank you for last night."

"The pleasure was all mine." Jo leaned down and kissed Ash briefly on the forehead. "I'm sorry, I really have to go. Later."

Ash watched her leave then picked up the mug. Later. She liked the sound of that.

There was no sign of anyone in the house when Ash finally made it downstairs. Not even a cat to be seen. She checked out the contents of the fridge. There was a small bowl of brown mush. On closer inspection she realized it was leftover cottage pie. The brown stuff was the lentils. It tasted good when it was hot, so she decided to give it a try. The first spoonful was heavenly and before she knew it the bowl was empty. Ash looked around the empty kitchen guiltily. She hoped Ellie hadn't been saving the cottage pie for something. Getting rid of the evidence seemed like a good plan so she washed and dried the spoon and the bowl and put them away.

Venturing outside, Ash saw the row of cars in front of the barn that indicated the arrival of Jo's pottery group. She wandered over to the chicken coop, breathing in the fresh air. The pecking of the hens was soothing to watch, but loud swearing suddenly disturbed the tranquil scene. Looking around she realized the noise could only have come from behind the building.

Robin was holding her arm and looking at the shovel lying on the ground in front of her.

"Hi. Got a problem?"

"Ground's too fucking hard. I can't make a dent in it. Nearly broke my arm."

"Need better equipment. Have you got a pickaxe?"

"No."

"Well, there's that tool hire place in town. You could try them."

Robin gave her an appraising look. "That's not a bad idea. Although a jackhammer's probably needed here. It's like concrete."

"We could go and see what they've got."

"We? You're planning on sticking around today."

"Sure. It's a day off and I've nothing else to do." Ash didn't mention that she was mainly looking forward to the "later" that Jo had promised.

"Okay. Great. I'll just go and get my wallet."

†

The trip into town took longer than Robin would have liked, but Ash had insisted they buy safety goggles and masks, so they had to make an extra trip to the nearest hardware store. Since it was mid-morning and she had been

213

up early, Robin suggested they stop off at Sainsbury's for a bacon sandwich. Ash confessed to finishing off the leftover lentils for breakfast.

"You are definitely in need of sustenance, then. You're not a veggie, are you?"

"No. I don't eat a lot of red meat though, mainly fish and chicken."

"Well, bacon doesn't count as red meat."

While they were eating, Robin took the opportunity to talk to the police officer about Jo. "Look, I don't want to come across as a heavy-handed parent, and Jo's no teenager, but I hope your intentions are honorable. She's had enough shit from other women in her life."

Ash gave her a steely blue-eyed stare that no doubt frightened the lowlife she was used to dealing with. "Does that include you?"

Robin stared back, chewing her bacon thoroughly before swallowing. "That was a one-off. And it was never going to be anything else. Jo knew that. She only came to the farm initially because she wanted to learn how to make pots."

"So you've not got some kind of threesome thing going at the farm?"

"I can't believe you said that!" Robin choked on a piece of bacon.

Ash smiled. "Just pulling your chain." She waited until Robin stopped spluttering to add, "Anyway, I've seen how you are with Ellie. You'd be nuts to cheat on her, wouldn't you?"

"I was nuts, for a while." Robin drank some coffee to soothe her throat. "But that's in the past. We're married now and Ellie means everything to me."

†

When they got back to the farm, Robin was ready to attack the hard packed ground behind the chicken coop but Ash put a restraining hand on her arm.

"Have you ever used one of these?" she asked.

Robin tightened her grip on the pickaxe. "No."

"Well, you look like you're going to chop your foot off. Let me show you."

Reluctantly, Robin let Ash take the heavy tool from her. After carefully adjusting her goggles and facemask, the police officer lifted the axe above her head and, with one smooth movement, landed a hefty blow on the compacted soil. Robin leapt back as shards of dirt flew up. Now she understood the need for the safety equipment.

Ash pulled her mask away from her mouth. "It looks like it's softer underneath this layer. How big an area do we need to clear?"

"Well, the width of the building and about six feet back."

"Okay, I'll do this strip here, then you can take over. Have you got a wheelbarrow to take away the rubble?"

"Yeah."

They worked together and, within half an hour, had stripped off the top layer of solid earth, working up a sweat in spite of the autumnal chill in the air.

Robin looked with satisfaction at the dark soil now showing. "Excellent! We we can start digging."

"Do you really expect to find anything under here?" Ash had removed her goggles and was wiping sweat from her forehead.

"Absolutely. If Ellie says this is the place, then I'm happy to go with it. Anyway, I think we've earned ourselves a beer. How about we take a break?"

†

The cars had gone from the farmyard and Ellie and Jo were in the kitchen making sandwiches when Ash and Robin arrived.

"Hey, we were going to bring these out to you," Ellie said.

Robin reached into the fridge and pulled out two bottles of beer. "Thirsty work."

"How was the class?" Ash asked Jo.

"They all said they would come back next week, so I guess it was all right."

"It was excellent." Ellie gave Jo's arm a squeeze. "She's a natural."

Jo blushed. "Well, I had a good teacher."

Ash excused herself to go and wash her hands. It was happening faster than she could have predicted. She didn't know if it was the atmosphere at the farm or the fact that her feelings for Jo deepened each time she saw her. Last night, it wasn't just the release of sexual tension, it was the warmth that crept into her soul just holding the woman in her arms. It was Jo's hair tickling her nose, the softness of her lips when they kissed. It was everything she'd thought she could never experience again.

Ash finished washing her hands and grimaced at her dirt-streaked face in the mirror. What on earth did Jo see in her? A damaged creature that needed rescuing, like Harry? She hoped there was more to it than that. Although Harry was obviously well loved.

Ash cleaned her face as best she could and went back into the kitchen. A plate stacked with healthy looking sandwiches graced the middle of the table. The other three women were already eating. It looked like Robin had washed her hands but hadn't bothered with anything else.

"I understand you two have been pigging out, literally," Ellie commented as she sat down.

"Yes. I didn't think I'd feel hungry again so soon, but these sandwiches look great." Ash took a long swig of the beer, welcoming the coolness.

"So you've cleared away the hard stuff."

"Yeah, now you girls can do the easy bit." Robin winked at her. The other two were obviously used to Robin's teasing and didn't rise to the bait.

"What do we do if we actually find anything?" Jo asked.

"We call Kathryn." Robin said, firmly.

†

Maybe a landscape archaeologist could make sense of it. That was Kathryn's first thought as she paced around the area. It wasn't much to go on. Just the imaginings of a disturbed artist. She didn't like to think that maybe Ellie was deranged. This whole thing about hearing the Queen speaking to her, appearing in her dreams. It was crazy. Why were they even doing this?

She glanced at the others. They were just enjoying a day out in the countryside. Den was waving her arms around, no doubt filling their visitors in on the history of the place. Steph was looking more interested than Jasmine, but that wasn't surprising. The gardener would at least appreciate the surrounding flora.

Had there been an Iron Age settlement here? She could access the university's archives to see if there had been any exploration of this place. Stanwick in North Yorkshire was the most famous site uncovered that was speculated to have been a Brigantes stronghold.

The pinging sound of her phone broke into her thoughts. She pulled it out of her pocket and looked at the screen. A text from Robin. When she opened it, the message just said, *call me.*

Kathryn walked further away from the others and made the call. Robin answered right away.

"Hi. I didn't want to disturb you if you're in a lecture."

"It's okay. I'm standing in the middle of a field. What's up?"

"We think we've found something. I'm going to email you a photo. See what you think."

"Are you sending it now?" Kathryn felt a chill down her spine.

"Yes."

"Okay. I'll check it out and call you back."

The email came through immediately and Kathryn waited impatiently for the photo to download. At least there was decent signal strength in this place. The image that came through was very clear. She recognized the object for what it was. The lead casing was distinctive.

She called Robin back. "Can you leave it as it is now? Cover it up with something. I can be with you tomorrow morning. Nine, latest." She didn't wait for confirmation, ending the call abruptly. Fridays she didn't have any lectures, and the only meeting she had arranged could be rescheduled. There was no point rushing over to Starling Hill now, it would be dark by the time they got there.

Trying to contain her bubbling excitement, she walked slowly back towards the others. Steph and Jas were planning to head back to London in the morning. Kathryn decided she would keep this news to herself until she and Den were alone.

Chapter Nine

Den glanced down at the kitten asleep on the folded blanket between her feet. Surprisingly, she'd slept all the way on the early morning drive to Starling Hill. Kathryn had been adamant about not leaving Misty behind.

The professor's strange behavior on the way back from Aldbrough St John had puzzled her. Kathryn cried off going out for a final dinner with Steph and Jas saying she had some work to catch up on. Den spent the evening with the two Londoners and said her goodbyes to them when they left the restaurant. She'd hardly touched any food, afraid of what she was going to find when she returned home.

Den was relieved to see no suitcases by the door when she got back to the flat. Instead, she found Kathryn pacing around the living room with Misty chasing shadows in a corner of the room.

"Do you want to tell me what's going on?"

"They've found it." Kathryn's face was alight with excitement.

"Who's found what?" Realization dawned even as she said the words. "They've found the coins."

"Yes. I'm going there tomorrow. Look." Kathryn snatched up her phone and quickly found the photo. "Robin sent this earlier."

Den looked at the partially uncovered object. It didn't look like anything to get excited about. "She sent you this when? While we were out? Why didn't you tell me then?"

Kathryn avoided her eyes, picking Misty up off the floor and stroking her gently.

"Oh, I get it. You didn't trust me not to blab to the others."

"No point turning it into a media circus until we know exactly what's there." Kathryn looked up at her. "I'm sorry, Den. Will you come with me?"

"Do you want me to?"

Kathryn put the now sleeping kitten on her chair and moved in close. "Of course I do. I want to share this with you. That's why I didn't say anything earlier. Jas and Steph would have wanted to be involved as well. There's no need for a whole troupe of us turning up at the farm."

Protecting Ellie, as usual. That would be first and foremost in the professor's mind. Den succeeded in tamping down the surge of jealousy that threatened to spill out. Instead, she pulled Kathryn into her arms and kissed her, transforming the negative feeling into the intense desire to take her to bed.

Now as they turned into the lane to the farm, Den could feel the excitement bubbling through her lover and she smiled at the memory of their passionate lovemaking the night before. If finding a few coins could ignite such fervor, she would happily start digging this hole herself.

†

Jo sighed as Harry snuffled contentedly next to her. She was warmed by his furry presence but she already missed Ash. The police officer was on the early shift and she'd had to go home to get a clean uniform shirt as well as a change of underwear. The five-thirty wakeup call had been unwelcome in many ways for Jo, and saying goodbye to her new lover was the worst.

"I'll be back this afternoon. I wish I could be here when they dig that thing up." Ash kissed her lightly on the forehead and then she was gone. Harry had nosed his way past her when she opened the bedroom door.

Sleep didn't return easily after Ash left. The events of the last few days made it hard for Jo's mind to settle down. Thoughts and images swirled around—the unfolding sweetness of making love with Ash, her first pottery class as the instructor, and then the imminent discovery of what might prove to be a valuable treasure trove.

The evening before had been strange. Robin was in a hyper mode so Ellie told her to take a bike ride. Ellie had been quieter than usual and, sensing she wanted to be alone with her thoughts, Jo suggested to Ash that they go over to the pottery studio. She wanted to do another check on how each of her students had progressed and plan the next session. Ash helped her tidy up and waited patiently while she made some notes. Jo had turned off the light, ready to leave, when Ash pulled her into an embrace and kissed her. If it hadn't been for the hard stone pressing into her back and the cold starting to seep into her bones, they would have made love right there. Fortunately, Ash agreed with moving to somewhere more comfortable, and they raced each other laughingly across the farmyard.

The bike was back and no one to be seen or heard in the living room, so it seemed Robin and Ellie had the same idea for an early night. Both cats were in the kitchen sleeping but when Harry started to follow them up the stairs, Jo had to tell him to stay. He flopped down, disappointed, gazing up at her with his head between his paws.

"Tomorrow, we'll have a nice long walk," she told him.

"I guess he must hate me," Ash whispered when they reached the bedroom door.

"Oh, he'll be fine." Jo had almost said, *he knows it's only temporary*. She hoped it wasn't true, this time.

†

Ellie woke up to the sound of a car's engine moving away from the house. Ash, she realized after a moment's thought. She had told them at dinner the night before that she was on the day shift but hoped to be back by three thirty. With the help she'd given Robin in digging out the trench, the police officer was as excited as any of them to find out what lay hidden in the ground.

Rolling over to move closer to Robin, Ellie wanted the comfort of her lover's warm body as she felt her peaceful world slipping away. If the hoard of coins was anything like the size the Queen said it was, their lives wouldn't be their own for some time to come. More coach parties would be turning up along with the world's media. Once the find was made public, the craziness would begin.

She felt Robin stir and opened her eyes to find the bright green ones gazing at her. Robin's sensitivity to her moods these days continually surprised her. Last night, returning from the bike ride, she had been tender with her, sensing Ellie just wanted to be held. She rolled over now and twined their legs together. Ellie could feel both their hearts beating as they lay in a conjoined embrace, as close as they could be without being inside each other's skin.

"Make love to me now," Ellie whispered. Without seeing her lover's face, she could feel the grin those words would elicit.

"Mm" was the only vocal response she got as Robin moved an arm so that she could cup one of Ellie's breasts in her hand.

Ellie moaned knowing that Rob's tongue, presently circling an earlobe would be travelling down to her breasts, then her belly and then her already throbbing clit. She circled her thighs in anticipation, the wetness seeping onto the leg trapped there.

The yowling of a cat brought Ellie out of her post-sex haze. Glancing at the bedside clock she was amazed to see it was after seven thirty.

"Rob!" Her lover was dozing lightly.

"What?"

"Time to get up. We've got animals to feed as well as ourselves, before our visitors arrive." Ellie didn't want to spoil the moment by mentioning Kathryn's name.

"Shower."

"Yes. But one at a time. No lingering. We don't need any more distractions this morning."

Robin leaned over her, resting on her elbow. "Am I just a distraction?"

"You are one very big distraction," Ellie managed to say before Robin covered her mouth with her own. She pulled away, laughing.

"All right. I'll go get the eggs while you shower." Robin hopped out of bed.

Ellie watched her pulling on her jeans over her slim hips and felt desire rush through her again.

Robin grinned at her mischievously as she lifted her arms to slip into a sweatshirt. "I know what you're thinking, Miss Winters," she said, as her head poked through the top. "But you will just have to wait." She walked out of the door with the cocky swagger of a woman who knew she had achieved top marks in her chosen subject.

Ellie was still smiling when she arrived in the kitchen ten minutes later. Showered and dressed she felt ready to face the day and whatever it might bring. Robin placed the basket of eggs on the counter by the door and pounded up the stairs to the bathroom. Her excitement was infectious and Ellie could finally feel enthusiasm for the day's activities.

†

The car had barely come to a stop when Kathryn opened her door and stepped out into the farmyard. Den climbed out more slowly, shaking her long limbs after their confinement during the two-hour drive. Misty looked up at her with a sleepy gaze from the footwell.

"Okay, munchkin. I'm not sure what we're going to do with you."

"She'll be fine there for now," Kathryn started to unload her equipment from the boot.

"I don't think she should stay in here. If she gets bored, she'll start ripping the upholstery. Anyway, she probably needs a pee and a drink. Like me."

"You've got your camera?"

Den sighed. Kathryn had asked her that several times before they set off at the crack of dawn.

"Yes. I'll take Misty inside and see if there's any coffee going." Den lifted the kitten out of her warm nest and was rewarded with a nip on her fingers. "Keep your hair on, fur ball. Come and meet your Auntie Ellie." She collected her camera case from the back seat before setting off to the house.

Ellie was in fact pouring out mugs of coffee when Den arrived in the kitchen. She said without turning around, "I heard the car. Thought you might need some refreshment."

"If you ever divorce Robin, I'll marry you." Den balanced the kitten in one hand and grasped a mug in the other.

Ellie glanced around at her. "Good drive? Oh, my, what's this?" She reached out to stroke Misty's head. The little cat purred.

"Guess she likes you. This is Misty. She was abandoned and Kathryn took her in." Den let Ellie take the kitten and concentrated on her coffee.

"She's a sweetie."

"Don't let her innocent look fool you. She'll chew anything that's left at floor level."

"Where's Kathryn?"

"Probably three feet down a trench by now."

"Robin's already out there. I was going to take her a coffee as well. Would Kathryn want one?"

"I think she's too wound up to want anything right now, other than seeing what's in your hole." Den flushed bright red as she realized what she'd said. "Sorry, I didn't mean…"

Ellie laughed. "I know what you meant. Let's go and see what they're doing. I think Misty will be okay in here."

"She might pee on the floor."

"Well, it won't hurt the flagstones." She handed Den another mug and grabbed the other two off the counter. "Come on. We don't want to miss the action."

†

Kathryn rounded the side of the chicken enclosure and discovered Robin and Jo staring down at the ground. Robin looked up at her approach.

"Morning, Professor. We've just taken the tarp off. Didn't want any curious creatures burrowing around during the night."

"Excellent." Kathryn surveyed the cleared area, noting the amount of earth that had been moved. "You did all this yourself?" She placed the theodolite case carefully on the ground.

"No. I had help from Jo's girlfriend." Robin ignored Jo's reddening cheeks. "Oh, I think you've met her. She's the police officer who showed up last time you were here."

"Well, that's great. You've both done a good job. Very tidy."

"Did Den come with you?" Jo asked.

"Yes. She's going to take photos so we have a visual record."

"And here she is, bearing coffee." Den approached, followed closely by Ellie. Den handed her extra mug to Kathryn. Ellie passed the other two to Robin and Jo.

"So, where do we start?" Robin asked.

"I'll set up the equipment first. I just need to work out the placement for the best angle. Den, could you get the measuring staff from the car? Oh, and there's a couple of buckets and kneeling mats in there as well."

Kathryn handed Jo her coffee and set about opening up the case. She was oblivious to any other activity around her as she paced out the area to find the right place for the tripod. When she was satisfied with the camera angle, she instructed Robin to hold the staff, resting lightly on the lead object. Den took photos, following the briefing Kathryn had given her on the drive to the farm.

Finally she was satisfied with the recording process. "Okay. Now, let's see what we've got." It was hard to keep the building excitement out of her voice. Finding the odd coin on the digs she'd been part of usually just helped date the site. Most of the time, the find was only part of a scattering of coins that had been inadvertently or carelessly dropped by their owners. The discovery of treasure hoards wasn't usually part of an archaeological venture. More often, they were the province of amateurs with metal detectors or unsuspecting farmers ploughing fields to plant crops.

Kathryn knelt down by the object and started to scrape away the excess dirt gently with her trowel. After a few minutes, she shifted uneasily on her mat. "This is bigger than I thought," she muttered to herself. She continued scraping, moving her mat several times as she uncovered more of the casing.

A collective sigh from the watchers brought her out of her reverie. She looked up at them. "This is big. It's going to take some shifting if it's full of coins."

†

Her phone rang just as they joined the M1, hoping for a clear run down the motorway to London. Steph was concentrating on maneuvering the van into the middle lane. "Take it if you want," she said, turning the volume down on the radio.

Jasmine looked at the screen and saw Henry's face.

"Hi."

"Where are you?" he asked, without preamble.

"Heading south on the M1, finally." It had been a long slow crawl down the mainly single track A1M even though they had managed to make an early start.

"Well, I think you should stay up north."

"What? Why?"

"Someone's watching our house. We're sure of it. The same car's been parked opposite for a few days now. It has tinted windows so we can't see who is inside. They move off when a traffic warden appears, but then they're back again."

"Shit! I guess Fitz's little ruse didn't put her off." Jas hadn't told Henry and Paul the full story about Max. Before they'd set off on their trip, she had just said that if a woman turned up asking about her or Steph to say they didn't live there.

"What's going on, Jas?"

"It's a long story. But I think you should phone the police."

"Can you give me a name, at least?"

"The car is likely either owned or hired by Max Fleetwood. The occupant may not be her. She has a PA called Roisin. Tall, blonde, Australian."

"Okay. So, where are you?"

Jas looked at Steph. "Where are we?"

"Coming up to Wakefield."

"Did you hear that? Near Wakefield."

"Well, do you think you could find a place to hang out for a bit? I'll see what kind of response I get from the cops. But don't hold your breath that they'll do anything."

Jas agreed and ended the call. "Where on earth are we going to 'hang out' around here?"

"We could go back up to Starling Hill. At least we know we'll get a decent cup of coffee there."

†

While she could appreciate the archaeologist's need for painstaking care, Robin found the waiting unbearable. The bagging and recording of a number of smaller items meant that the whole process had taken two hours already. Jo and Ellie had gone into the studio. Den went off to make more coffee, but only when Kathryn said she didn't need a photo taken for a while.

The evidence of a hypocaust excited Kathryn, and she explained the context in more detail than Robin wanted. She'd thought the piles of stones were just randomly placed, but when the professor measured the distances between them and made a quick sketch, she could see they were part of a carefully engineered structure.

"They knew from experience that in our damp climate, they had to keep the grain dry during the winter months. So this under-floor heating system is as well constructed as any they would have used for their own villas."

Robin was relieved when Kathryn finally stopped making notes and said they could try lifting the lead casket now. The trench was three feet deep and Den helped the professor climb out. The three of them stood looking down at the container.

"Why would they have used lead?" Robin asked.

"It wouldn't rot away like leather. Although the anaerobic conditions of the soil here would have been protection enough. But they wouldn't have known that."

"But why lead?"

"Lead mining was taking place here well before the Romans arrived. Obviously they took it to a new level, needing it for pipes and so on."

"Guess they didn't know about the long term dangers of using lead piping, then."

"So, how are we going to get this thing out without damaging it?" Den asked.

"A pulley system."

They all turned to look at the new speaker. Steph was looking into the hole with her hands on her hips.

"Hi, folks. Unplanned detour. But it looks like you need some expert help. I've got rope in the van. And we'll need a few planks to roll it up with."

Robin offered to see what she could find in the barn. As she walked away with the gardener, she heard Jas saying to Den, "I knew you were keeping something back. Why didn't you tell me?"

"I didn't know until I got home from the restaurant."

Once they were out of earshot, Robin turned to Steph. "So, what happened? I thought you were on your way back to London?"

"Henry phoned. He thinks Max has the house staked out."

"Jesus! What's up with the woman?"

"Beats me." Steph grimaced. "Sorry, poor choice of words. Anyway, Henry thought we should stay out of the way for a bit longer." She opened the back doors of her van. It was empty apart from the suitcase and a large coil of heavy looking rope.

Robin waited for her to haul it out. "Don't you have any tools? You know, gardening stuff."

"Sure. But I left it all at Henry's." She closed the doors again and pointed to the small sign at the bottom of the right hand door. *No tools left overnight.* "Fact of life these days. That's why I don't have any advertising on the van either."

With Steph's help, they made short work of moving the lead case out of the trench. Robin was impressed by the gardener's know-how as she fashioned a rope cradle for the container and positioned the planks she'd found to make a ramp. Then the two of them could then haul it up onto level ground. By now Jo and Ellie had joined them to see what was going on.

Den photographed each stage of the removal. As soon as it was out, Kathryn jumped back down into the hole to explore the cavity left behind.

Steph was asking if there might be a cup of coffee on offer, or maybe something stronger as it was now near lunchtime, when the professor let out a yell.

"There's another one!"

Robin could see that she had only scraped a thin layer with her trowel and there was more lead showing through. Ellie had moved close to her and she put a comforting arm around her shoulders. Robin knew that while it was an exciting adventure for the rest of them, Ellie was struggling with the idea of any more notoriety coming their way.

"This is obviously going to take a while. Why don't we break for lunch?" Robin looked around at the group. "I'll take orders for pizzas and go and collect them."

There were murmurs of assent from everyone except the professor who was still scraping away in the trench. Den winked at Robin. "It's okay. I'll order for her."

†

Ash sat back in her seat. Taking one look when she arrived at the station for their shift, Ross had offered to drive.

"Looking a bit peaky. You okay?"

"Sure. Never better." Ash smiled at him, but handed over the keys without any argument. She wasn't sure how she had managed to drive back to her house and then on to the station. It was all a blur. Her mind was still on the last two nights spent with Jo.

"You'll know when you meet the right person," were the words offered by the therapist at one of her counseling sessions after Cos's death. Ash had told her she didn't think she would ever fall in love again. The devastating loss was too painful. The counselor's words hadn't registered at the time. No one could ever replace Cos.

It was true that no one could ever replace Cos, but the last two nights had proved that Ash was capable of loving someone again.

"Earth to Ash." Ross's voice entered her head.

"Sorry, what?"

"You were miles away."

Ash looked at him. He was a nice guy, but she wasn't ready to share her innermost feelings with him. It was all too new. Along with the love was the fear that it would be snatched away from her. The fear was that maybe Jo wasn't in love with her, but was just being kind, knowing that she needed something to help her move beyond her grief for Cos.

"I'm the passenger so I get to zone out while you drive."

It had been a quiet day on the roads giving Ash plenty of time to zone out. She had spent most of the shift fantasizing about asking Jo to move in with her. She could see them as a happy family, herself and Jo and Harry. Was it just wishful thinking? She wouldn't know unless she asked, but Ash wasn't sure she should ask. The counselor hadn't given any advice on what to do when she did meet the right person.

The farmyard had more vehicles in it than when she'd left that morning. A white van and the red Honda Civic she'd seen before. She could hear voices coming from the direction of the chicken coop.

The scene that met her eyes was like something out of a gruesome thriller. She'd never seen an exhumation other than on the occasional TV cop show, but that's what it looked like. Robin and another woman were hauling on a rope, which was being guided out of a now very deep hole by the shorter of the two women she'd caught making out in the barn before. Her partner, the tall one, was photographing the event, flashes from the camera lending an additional eerie quality to the scene in the rapidly approaching dusk.

"What's happening?" she asked another woman she'd not seen before who was standing back from the group.

"This is the third one they've pulled out."

"Third what?"

"Lead casing. Full of coins."

"How do they know? Have they opened them up?"

"Not yet. Dr. Moss says we have to wait for the FLO."

"The what?"

"Finds Liaison Officer."

"Of course."

Ash felt the sudden warmth as a body nestled up behind her, arms reaching around to pull her close. A surge of delight gripped her as Jo whispered in her ear, "Hey, sexy. When did you get here?"

Resisting the urge to grind her hips into Jo's pelvis, she whispered back, "Just now." And just as suddenly the fears she'd been nurturing all day melted into the gathering gloom. Tonight she would ask. It felt right.

†

Somehow it was reminiscent of Jasmine's first visit to the farm. The time when she thought she would be spending an idyllic week in the arms of her lover, Robin.

A mere eighteen months earlier, Jasmine had been sitting in this very room, listening to Jo strumming on her guitar, with the dawning realization that Robin wouldn't easily be pried away from either the farm or Eleanor Winters. Kathryn had been there then as well—the visit that had precipitated the dig leading to the discovery of Queen Cartimandua's bones.

Jas had thought they were all crazy then, and it was almost as insane now. The discussions over an Indian takeaway meal had centered on what the coins could be worth. She leaned back against the sofa and relaxed into Steph's strong fingers massaging her neck, while the professor lectured on the subject, cradling a sleepy kitten in her arms.

"Depends what denominations we find. Dating will be fairly easy if they're Roman. The emperors Claudius and Nero were both in power during Cazza's reign. Brigantes' minted coins would be a massive bonus. They would be worth a lot."

Robin looked up from her iPad. "The Frome hoard was worth over three hundred thousand pounds. Fifty-two thousand coins mostly made from bronze or debased silver, it says here."

Kathryn nodded. "Yes. I don't think we'll have that many. We have to take into consideration the weight of the containers. However, as they've gone to the trouble of encasing them in lead and burying them in a deep pit, we can probably be fairly sure they are high denomination. Cazza, as chief of the tribe, would have been able to skim off some hefty profits. Although not a lot is known about her reign, there is evidence the Brigantes had been doing business with Roman traders long before the legions turned up. "

"You make her sound quite mercenary," Ellie said quietly.

"Well, as has been said, 'power corrupts, absolute power corrupts absolutely'." Den offered.

"I don't think of her that way." Ellie reiterated more strongly.

"Don't forget, she was ousted and no doubt felt betrayed by people who had been close to her. She would have wanted to hurt them in some way. If she couldn't defeat her enemies in battle, maybe she wanted to disable them financially."

Ellie smiled at Den. "Maybe. That's as good an explanation as any." She stood and started clearing the empty plates and cartons. Robin jumped up to help her.

Jas had to admit the two of them worked well together. Robin seemed to be taking her marital status seriously.

†

"I don't know where everyone will sleep." Ellie said as she switched on the taps to fill the sink.

239

"I've got a suggestion."

Ellie turned, surprised to see Ash.

"Jo and I can go back to my house for the night. I've got a guest room so two more could join us."

"That would be great." Ellie smiled at her. "Thank you for offering. I guess, if you don't mind, Kathryn and Den could go with you. Then we just need to change the sheets on Jo's bed."

"Sure. If you tell me where to find clean ones, I'm happy to do that."

"Jo can show you. She'll probably need to take a few things with her."

"Okay. What time is the finds person showing up?"

"Kathryn said ten was the earliest they could get here."

Robin looked over from the table where she was clearing the food cartons into a plastic bag. "I think the professor would like to sleep with the containers."

"I know." Ellie put a few plates into the washing up bowl. "I'm surprised she didn't break one of them open. She could have told the FLO it broke while being moved."

"Too many witnesses," Ash said.

"Absolutely." Robin gave her a lopsided grin. "She probably thinks you're a police spy."

"Right, well I'll go and get the bedroom sorted with Jo."

Ellie turned back from the sink. "Ash, thanks for everything. I haven't had the chance to thank you properly for helping Rob yesterday." She walked over, her hands still wet, and kissed Ash on the cheek. The police officer blushed and backed out of the room.

Robin hugged Ellie from behind. "I think you embarrassed her, love."

†

Everyone was settled in for the night, including Harry. Ash had insisted he come with them. She had also told Kathryn it was fine to bring Misty. The enclosed back garden would be safe to let her out to do her business.

Jo thought the professor didn't look too happy about having to leave the farm. When Ash was giving her directions to her house, Kathryn just told her testily to give her the postcode and she would find it. And the Honda had pulled into Ash's drive a few minutes after they arrived.

Harry happily explored the garden while Ash showed Den and Kathryn where they were sleeping. When he'd finished marking his territory, Jo called him in. She explained that he would have to stay in the kitchen and he accepted his fate when she placed his blanket on the floor. She'd brought it from the van, along with his water and food bowls.

Ash was standing by the window in the bedroom when Jo entered, seemingly engrossed by the nighttime view of her garden. Jo stood next to her. It was too dark to see anything outside. Ash had been quiet all evening, not that she was generally noisy, but it was a different kind of quiet.

"Do you want to talk about it?" Jo asked, not sure what *it* might be.

Ash nodded.

"Let's sit down, then." Jo guided her gently over to the bed. They sat, side by side.

Jo waited, and after a few minutes, Ash reached over and took one of Jo's hands in her own. She looked at Jo, blue eyes searching her face, brow furrowed.

"What's the matter?"

"I know this is probably too soon." Ash looked away from her again. "We've only spent a few nights together. But how would you feel about moving in with me?"

Whatever she had thought Ash was going to say, this wasn't even close. Jo looked down at their entwined hands.

"I know it's too early to even think we're in love, but I want to give it a try."

"I don't have a very good track record, Ash. Most of my previous girlfriends have left me after a few months."

"Well, I'm not going anywhere. If you moved in here, you would be the one who could leave, whenever you wanted to."

Jo smiled to herself. Was it really only a few months ago she'd been sitting in the barge offering chamomile tea and relationship advice to a lovelorn Den, acting like some wise old herbalist? She didn't feel very wise now.

"What are you thinking, Jo?"

"I was thinking I'd like a cup of chamomile tea."

"What?" Ash looked stricken.

"I'm sorry, Ash." Jo gazed into her eyes and stroked her cheek. "I would love to move in here. But I do think it's a bit premature. We hardly know each other."

"I'm good at reading people. It goes with the job. Being with you, it feels right to me."

"It feels right to me, too. I'm not saying, no. I'm just saying maybe we should give it a bit more time."

"How much time?"

Jo moved in for a kiss. After savoring the sweetness of Ash's lips for a few minutes, she pulled back. "Is next Tuesday too soon?"

†

"I don't see why we couldn't have stayed at the farm? We hardly know these two."

Den placed the towels Ash had given her onto the bed, and then pulled Kathryn down beside her.

"Well, I think it's perfectly understandable. I've slept in that room at the farmhouse and believe me, you wouldn't want to be there."

"Why? What's wrong with it?"

"God, Kathryn, for a professor you can be a bit dim at times. Do you think the walls are soundproof? Ellie was only trying to spare your feelings."

Misty made a mewling sound in Kathryn's arms.

"See. She agrees. We're fine here. It's only a half-hour drive and we'll leave in the morning as soon as we get up." Den looked at the kitten. "Does she need to go outside?"

"Probably." Kathryn was looking at the floor.

"Okay. I'll take her. You get to use the bathroom first." Den kissed the top of her head and took the kitten out of her arms. "Come on, fur ball. We've got a date."

When she returned, Kathryn was already in bed with her eyes closed. Den knew she wasn't asleep but she quietly put the kitten in the basket they'd brought with them and got herself ready for bed. Walking back from the bathroom, she could hear Ash and Jo talking in the other bedroom, their door ajar. No doubt waiting for their guests to settle down. She moved past quietly and returned to the guest room. Misty was curled up in her basket, already asleep, worn out with all the day's new experiences.

Kathryn, on the other hand, was very much awake. She didn't say anything until Den crawled into bed and spooned her body next to her.

"You got some good photos, didn't you?"

"You know I did." Den had downloaded them onto her laptop while they waited for Robin to return from the Indian takeaway, and they'd all had a look.

"Ellie's not very happy, is she?"

Den sighed and stroked the professor's leg. "No, I don't suppose she is. If these coins turn out to be as valuable as you suspect, it turns her world upside down again."

"Well, it's her fault."

"How do you reckon that?"

"If she hadn't been communing with Cazza…not that I believe any of that nonsense for a second…"

"How do you explain the fact that they knew exactly where to dig?"

"Mmm…well…"

"Mmm…yes. Ellie could have not told anyone, kept it to herself. But she wanted to do right by the queen. And the queen wants a reburial, like Richard III."

"Oh, right. Next you'll be saying Cartimandua's been watching the news."

"You must have believed some of what Ellie told us. Why bother with the trip to Aldbrough St John, if you didn't think there was something in it?"

Kathryn turned towards her. "I don't think I'll be able to sleep tonight."

Den pulled her in close, enjoying the softness of Kathryn's breasts meeting hers. "Who said anything about sleeping?"

†

The light from the bedside lamp threw eerie shadows across the low-beamed room. Jasmine crawled across the bed into the waiting arms of her lover. She stroked the tattoo on Steph's forearm, a delicate trail of petals from Jas's namesake flower. When Steph told her about the design she was having inked a few weeks earlier, Jas had been delighted. Steph had teased that she couldn't go with a big red heart reading "I love Jasmine" in the middle.

"My white-van-woman," Jas said now as she snuggled close.

"You don't wish you were next door with Robin?"

Jas pulled herself up to look into Steph's eyes. "You're just fishing for compliments now."

"So, do you think Den's friend can pull it off?"

During the lunch break earlier in the day, Jasmine had talked to Den about Henry's house being watched. "Den says Fitz has contacts at several of the tabloids. She'll do her best to plant something of a fairly explicit nature in at least one of their gossip columns tomorrow."

"That's great. But people like Max don't read the red-tops."

"Someone will see it and I'm sure she's made more than a few enemies in the business who will be only too happy to make sure the news spreads."

"I almost feel sorry for her."

"No, you don't." Jas kissed her and moaned into her mouth as Steph reached down to clasp her buttock with one hand while moving the other to caress the closest breast.

†

Robin stoked up the fire, putting another log on. Both cats were occupying the armchair, so she settled down on the sofa with Ellie curled up next to her.

"I'll just be glad when this is all over. I'm looking forward to Christmas with Aiden and Sophie, and Wren."

It would be Wren's first birthday as well as the first Christmas they could spend together as a family. Robin knew Ellie was looking forward to spoiling her granddaughter.

"Maybe they'll have more news for us, " Robin said, stroking the loose strands of Ellie's blonde hair away from her face.

"Yes, I'm hoping they'll get married soon."

That wasn't the news they were going to impart. Aiden had posted news of his partner's pregnancy on Facebook. Robin had sent him a private message telling him to phone his mother or she would rip his head off. He usually responded to Robin's not-so-idle threats.

A knock on the door startled them both just as they were settling into a more comfortable position. Robin removed her arm from around Ellie's shoulders, ready to get up, when they heard the front door open. Obviously it was someone who knew the door wouldn't be locked.

"Maybe the prof's forgotten something."

But it was the tall form of Dr. Ed who poked his head around the door.

"Hi, ladies. Sorry to call so late. May I come in?"

Ellie sat up. "Please do. Would you like a drink?"

"No thanks. I'm driving."

"Hey, a small glass of wine, at least." Robin got to her feet and gave Soames and Fleur the choice of moving or being moved. They both looked at her with undisguised loathing before stalking off.

"We were just going to have something," Ellie said. "We're waiting for the fire to die down before going to bed."

"Well, if you insist. Just a small red, Robin. And I mean small."

"Okay, doc. Keep your hair on. Back in a tick."

Robin returned with a tray that held a glass of white wine for Ellie, a full glass of red for herself, and a half glass for Ed. He was sitting in the armchair, oblivious to the murderous stare from the ginger cat now crouched next to the sofa.

"So, what brings you out here at this time of night?" Ellie asked.

"Well, I've got the results back from the DNA test."

"That's quick. I thought it would take weeks."

"Oh, we have our own lab connections." He took a sip of his wine before continuing. "It's definitely a match, Ellie. No doubt about it. You and Cartimandua could have been sisters."

Robin looked at Ellie and then back at Ed. "You're kidding me. How can you tell that after two thousand years?"

"It's about eighty percent accurate with just the mitochondrial DNA. Unless we find the bones of her father or brother, there's no way to quantify it."

"But, honestly, Ed. Half the population of the world could be related to Cartimandua." Ellie gave him what Robin called her stern-teacher look. "I've read about these genetics companies. Happy to take people's money just so they can say they're related to some historical figure. Might as well be Darth Vader or Bilbo Baggins. If Kathryn thinks she can use this result as a money-making scheme, count me out. I don't want any part of it."

Ed finished off his small portion of wine in one big gulp. He set the glass back down on the table, carefully.

"I fully understand. I did warn Kathryn I thought this was a bad idea." He pulled an envelope out of the inside pocket of his jacket. "I'll leave this with you. It's the report from the lab."

Robin pulled the paper out of the envelope and read it while Ellie saw Ed out.

"Are you really not bothered about this?" she asked, as Ellie sat down again and sipped at her wine.

"No."

"But…all this time…you've been hearing her voice…"

"I know. It might all be in my mind. I don't believe in this psychic stuff any more than you do, but I can't explain the painting or knowing where to look for the coins. Obviously, there is some kind of connection. Whether or not

I'm related to her isn't relevant. I feel committed now to making sure she is put to rest and given the burial she deserves."

Epilogue

Kathryn looked around at the assembled crowd. They were a mixed bunch. The academics were outnumbered about five-to-one by the Druids and representatives of other alternative religions. Most of her colleagues had atheistic leanings. She had been skeptical about involving the Druids, but Jo Bright Flame was adamant that not only should they be included, but should officiate the ceremony. Personally Kathryn thought the modern Druids had as much idea as she did about how burial rites would have been practiced two thousand years ago.

The idea of having the ceremony on the last day of April was entirely Ellie's. The ancient festival of Beltane traditionally took place on the eve of the first day of May—which marked the start of summer—fertility dances all round.

People had been arriving from midday onwards. Having acquired the necessary funding, Kathryn was pleased to see the queues outside the trailer set up for DNA testing at the edge of the field. Men and women alike seemed happy to pay the nominal five pound fee to find out if they were related to the first century queen, even if she had been outed as a lesbian.

Events had progressed surprisingly quickly after the discovery and valuation of the Starling Hill hoard. Ellie visited the site at Aldbrough St John and confirmed that it was the site the queen had specified. It had been an unnerving experience watching Ellie as she walked around with her eyes closed, Robin leading her. She stopped several times, head on one side, as if listening to something.

Then came the moment when she held up her hand and said, "This is it."

Another surprise had been the willingness of the owners of the field to have it developed into a permanent monument to Cartimandua. The final plans were still being discussed with the involvement of the British Museum and English Heritage, but there would soon be a full-fledged small museum built on the site. A sculptor was working on statues of the queen and Vellocatus to grace the entrance, a lasting memorial, with their names carved in stone. Ellie's original painting of the two women would be on display along with the other artefacts from the exhibition and some of the coins from the hoard.

The professor glanced down at the sapphire ring on her finger. Den had proposed again at Christmas and she'd accepted. She felt more comfortable with the idea now. The journalist materialized next to her, as if magically divining her thoughts. On a night like this she could almost believe in magic.

Kathryn looked up at her fiancée. "Do you think Misty will be all right at the farm?"

If Den was surprised that she was thinking of the kitten in the midst of the reburial ceremony, she didn't show it. "She loves it there and we're only going to be gone two weeks."

The following evening they were flying out to Australia where Kathryn had been invited to speak at a convention. The timing couldn't be better. She would now be able to incorporate the images from this event that was bringing closure to the Brigantes queen and her consort.

"Is Ellie here?"

"Yes. I saw her and Robin arrive some time ago. Do you want to join them?"

Kathryn leaned back against her lover. "No, I'm happy to stay here with you." As she spoke, the crowd in front of the bonfire linked arms and the chanting started.

†

Ellie smiled at Robin as the bonfire was lit and flames leapt upwards into the clear night sky. This was perfect—

exactly the kind of sendoff she had envisaged for the queen. A Beltane fire, dancing Druids, the low murmur from the crowd as a chant started.

When they began this journey, almost two years before with the finding of the first bone by Jo's dog, Harry, she couldn't have imagined this scene. And it was now almost six months to the day since they found the hoard of coins that had made so many things possible.

The building work at the farm was almost finished. Their tickets were booked for their trip across Russia on the Golden Eagle. They would be extending the journey with a visit to China—a walk along the Great Wall, a visit to see the Terra Cotta army, Beijing, Shanghai. So many places she could only have dreamed of seeing before.

The birth of her second grandchild was imminent. There was a chance they would still be on their travels when she was born, but Robin convinced her they would be able to Skype from wherever they were. After a heated discussion, Ellie had dissuaded Aiden from calling the child Cartimandua. He and Sophie were now favoring Cassandra.

†

Kieran Taylor parked next to the white van and surveyed the farmyard with dismay as he got out and looked around. Whatever now. He really shouldn't have extended his stay in Australia. Much as he'd enjoyed the time with his son's family, Ellie had obviously gone mad.

A strange woman approached, dark hair flopped over one eye, strong looking arms covered in tattoos emerging from a tank top.

"Can I help you?"

"Is Ellie here?" *God, I hope she hasn't sold up.*

"Not at the moment." She brushed the hair out of her eyes and peered at him. "They're on their way back from the burial though. Should be here by lunchtime."

"Burial? Who died?" His mind leapt to the few people he knew who were close to Ellie. Both her parents were dead. Robin, Aiden, little Wren.

The woman read the stricken look on his face and laughed. "No one you know. They're reburying the bones of Cartimandua and Vellocatus."

"Oh, right. Gosh. I'm sorry I missed that." He held out his hand. "I'm Kieran, by the way. An old friend. I'm also a potter."

"Steph. A not-so-old friend." She grinned at him and shook his hand. "Dog and cat sitter at the moment."

Kieran laughed. "So, what's going on here, Steph?"

"Ellie decided to put some of the money back into the house. There were some old plans for an extension lying around."

"It's pretty impressive. Is she starting a commune?"

"Sort of. There are six of us living here now. And we have room for a few guests."

"Where did the money come from?"

"Ah, well. That's a long story. I'm ready for a break. Do you fancy a beer?"

†

Leading the way into the new wing on the house, Steph considered what she should tell the old man with the long gray ponytail. He looked more like one of Jo's hippy friends than someone Ellie would hang out with. She grabbed two beers from the fridge in the new kitchen and took him out onto the deck that faced the field where it had all started. Uncapping the beers with her belt buckle, she handed one of the bottles to him and sat down on a chair.

He sat down next to her. "Did she win the lottery? This is amazing."

"I guess you could say that she did, in a way. A two-thousand-year-old lottery." Steph took a long swallow of beer. "Were you here when they uncovered the bones?"

"Yes. And I was at the opening of the exhibition at the museum last year. You were there, too, weren't you?" He was gazing at her intently.

"Yeah, I was. I don't remember seeing you there."

"I was in disguise." He patted his head. "I'd cut my hair in preparation for my trip to Australia."

"Oh, right. Well, it seems the queen was loaded. There was a massive stash of coins buried here."

Kieran leaned forward in his chair as Steph continued with the tale. She told him about hauling out the heavy lead containers, followed by the visit the next day from the local finds officer and an official from English Heritage. The excitement from that day would live in her memory forever. Each container held a great quantity of coins, too many to be counted there and then. When Ellie was informed of the results it was evident she was going to be very rich. One container held over twelve thousand gold aurei, all bearing the likeness of the emperor Claudius and twenty thousand denarii were in another container from Nero's era. But it was the third container that held the biggest surprise: more than ten thousand gold coins with Cartimandua's image. Finds of British coins were extremely rare, they were told by the experts. The hoard found not far away over a hundred years earlier had only yielded one silver coin with what they thought was an image of the Brigantes queen.

Steph sat back in her chair and chugged the rest of her beer. The old man was now staring off into the distance.

"A lot of changes," he said finally. "Who's living here now, then?"

"Well, there's Robin and Ellie, of course. You might know Jo, she also does pottery."

He nodded.

"So she and her girlfriend, Ash, moved in last month. Ash has a house in Honley, but she's renting it out. And Jas and I came up about the same time. We've moved from London. I'm a gardener so I can generally find work anywhere. And Jas is finding some PR work through contacts Robin has in Leeds and Manchester."

"What about the professor and her journalist friend?"

"Oh, they live in Durham. But they visit a lot. And they're engaged now. I think Den's hoping she can convince Kathryn to have the wedding here."

Kieran smiled at her. "It's a lovely place for a wedding. Mind you, the summers here are great when the sun shines and the wind dies down. You haven't been here for a winter yet. That sorts out the…ah…women from the girls."

"Oh I think we'll survive." She waved her empty bottle. "Another?"

†

Jo watched the movie clips on Robin's iPad. Ellie was driving so Robin kept turning around to check on her.

"These are great, Rob. I'm glad you managed to capture the Arch Druid's speech. I couldn't hear all of it from where I was."

"Shame Ash couldn't come."

"I know. But it just wasn't possible with her being on nights again now."

Jo was pleased with the way things had worked out. After those first few tentative nights with the police officer, their love was growing day by day. She had moved into Ash's house in November, and although she loved the deepening of their relationship, it had been hard traveling the extra miles to the market, then to Starling Hill for the pottery sessions, each time wondering if her old camper van would make it.

With the extension on the farmhouse nearing completion she had been delighted when Ellie invited them to move in. Of course, it had first to pass the police inspection to make sure it was a suitable place for an officer of the law to live. She had left the van parked at Ash's house that day.

The addition of Steph and Jasmine to the mix was working out as well. Although they had managed to shake off the unwelcome attention of Max Fleetwood, they both felt they were ready to leave London and try country living.

The only discomfort for Jo came when Ellie offered her a substantial sum of money after the valuation of the hoard.

"If it hadn't been for you and Harry, none of this would have even happened," Ellie said, trying to convince her to take the offer.

"I don't know. Kathryn had already done an aerial survey. That's why she came to the farm that night, to ask if they could dig there."

"Sure. But they might not have found the bones. Archaeologists don't usually go looking for skeletons. Finding old bones are generally more trouble than they're worth."

"Well, these skeletons were worth quite a lot. I'd rather you gave the money to charity."

Eventually they had settled on Ellie covering the costs of a new van after Robin told her the camper was on its last legs. Ellie had also been convinced the Jeep needed retiring and they were traveling in style now in the brand new Jeep Renegade.

The ceremony had been perfect. Jo was still on a high and looking forward to sharing the memories of the evening with Ash who would likely be awake when they got back. Jo glanced over at Jasmine who had been dozing for most of the journey. It was hard to believe this was the same woman who had shown up at the farm two years earlier, intent on taking Robin away. Jo could never have imagined that she and Jas would now be living on the farm with their respective lovers, all part of an extended family.

When they drove up the long lane and pulled into the farmyard, Ellie was the first to recognize the extra vehicle. "Kieran's here!" she shouted. Throwing the keys to Robin, she leapt out and ran into the house.

Jo laughed. "She's happy. You must be doing something right."

Robin went round to the back of the Jeep to retrieve their bags. "Nothing to do with me. She's just relieved it's all over. I don't think any of us realized how much it was weighing her down. The queen is at rest and now she's free."

The Last Word

Resting in Peace

I, Vellocatus, by royal command, thank you for the love and respect shown to my queen and myself.

The ceremony and preparations for the new temple—a permanent shrine to our everlasting love—is a fitting tribute to the Queen of the Brigantes, leader of the greatest tribe in Britain.

We would thank, first and foremost, the sweet woman—talented potter and painter—who has served the queen's wishes so well. She has been rewarded for her patience and persistence.

A great thank you also to the digger and her wordsmith consort for their assistance in giving Queen Cartimandua her due.

Above all, we are pleased to be home at last—our bones resting side by side in this double tomb.

Blessings on you all.

Jen Silver

About the Author

Jen Silver

Jen lives near Hebden Bridge in West Yorkshire with her long-term partner whom she married in December 2014. She has always enjoyed reading an eclectic range of genres including sci-fi, fantasy, historical fiction and lesbian fiction. As well as reading and writing, other activities include golf and archery. Her firsthand experience of an archaeological dig and a lifelong interest in Roman history were the creative forces behind her first published novel, *Starting Over,* released by Affinity in October 2014. The second book in the series, *Arc Over Time,* was published in May 2015 and the third book, *Carved in Stone,* in February 2016. Jen insists that she didn't set out to write a trilogy, but the characters demanded a proper conclusion to the story.

Contact Jen at jenjsilver@yahoo.co.uk, friend her on Facebook, or visit her blog: https://jenjsilver.wordpress.com.

Other Books from Affinity eBook Press

Bound by Ali Spooner
A rogue master vampire threatens the existence of the New Orleans vampire clan. Lord Jordan enlists Devin Benoit, sister of the Baton Rouge Alpha, and her witch lover, Tia, to assist with cleansing the city from potential disaster.

The Circle Dance by Jen Silver
Jamie Steele has moved to another town, trying to forget the heartbreak of losing her lover of six years. Sasha Fairfield finds her thoughts taken up with her ex-lover and thinks she wants Jamie back. Follow this captivating romance as love dances through the lives of these women to its surprising conclusion.

Search for the White Moon by Natalie London
Kathryn Austin, a government agent, is given opera singer, Adriana Desi, as her new assignment. Their lives and futures are in danger as the White Moon terrorists hunt them. Immerse yourself in this fast-paced romantic thriller by debut author Natalie London.

Take Me As I Am by JM Dragon & Erin O'Reilly
When Jo Lackerly and Thea Danvers meet, an unexpected friendship develops, proving a catalyst for both women to change their lives irrevocably. Follow them on a journey of discovery that will have your heart smiling, blood boiling, and senses entangled in a wonderful romance.

Carved in Stone by Jen Silver
Join the characters from *Starting Over* and *Arc Over Time* in this final book from the Starling Hill trilogy. Ellie Winters thinks she might be going mad when the ancient queen wants a proper burial for herself and her consort. *Carved in Stone* has romance, adventure, a treasure hunt, and a happy endings for all, living and dead.

Anywhere, Everywhere by Renee MacKenzie
Gwen Martin's life in the Ten Thousand Islands area changes irrevocably when Piper Jackson comes into her life. Without trust, can the budding relationship between Gwen and Piper survive? Or will the answers to the questions continue to haunt them?

Venus Rising by Ali Spooner
Levi Johnson arrives at Venus Rising, an exclusive lesbian-only tropical resort in the Virgin Islands and finds more than she expected—a sizzling hot love triangle. Torn between her attraction to two women, she struggles to choose the right woman to share her life.

The Devil's Tree by Ali Spooner

Torn between her love for the pack and her need to find what's missing in her life, Devin Benoit travels to New Orleans. Will the previous happenings at the Devil's Tree help or hinder Devin in the fight of her life, and the life of Tia, the woman who now owns her heart?

The Beggars' Coppice by Erica Lawson
Edda Case is a woman in crisis who discovers that things are not as they seem. Is it truly a message for her from beyond the grave or is something more sinister taking place? Can Edda solve the mystery of *The Beggars' Coppice*?

Locked Inside by Annette Mori
How much does the power of love matter to someone who must overcome obstacles far greater than most people face in a lifetime.

Line of Sight by Ali Spooner
Sasha and her lover Kara are back. Continue the thrilling adventures of this couple from the Sasha Thibodaux series.

Requiem for Vukovar by Angela Koenig
Requiem for Vukovar continues the Refraction series and the exploits of Jeri O'Donnell and her partner, Kelly Corcoran. In an epic siege largely ignored by the wider world, Kelly, who was prepared to give up comforts and certainties when she became part of Jeri's nomadic life, encounters more than physical danger. Her ability to maintain her core integrity is assaulted by the inevitable ugliness of war. For Jeri, the true battle is confronting her attraction to violence as she struggles against losing herself in the exhilaration of combat.

Jen Silver

Against All Odds by JM Dragon
From award-winning and bestselling author JM Dragon, with significant updates by Erin O'Reilly, comes an original tale of romance where everything seems to be stacked against two women whose destinies bring them together. Life however takes a twisted path, setting both Steph and Louise in directions they never thought possible. Will love win out against all odds or will love be forever lost?

The Settlement by Ali Spooner
The outpouring of love and friendship toward Cadin helps her on her path to healing and learning to trust her heart to love once again. Join bestselling author Ali Spooner on this sensational journey that ends with a heartwarming romance.

Once Upon a Time by Alane Hotchkin
Raven only wanted to escape the blows that life had dealt her. She longed to be on the open sea and free. When she came upon a beautiful young girl sitting alone in the middle of a meadow, little did she know that her destiny would be changed forever. Will they become the pawns of the ancient vision or will both paths lead to the same port of destiny? Find out in this exciting high seas adventure that will capture your imagination.

Asset Management by Annette Mori
Follow the twists and turns to the explosive conclusion. Not everything is black and white. There are many shades of gray, and sometimes it's difficult to decipher who is good

266

and who is evil. No one is all virtue or all malevolence, but sometimes love helps us rise above.

Do Dreams Come True? by JM Dragon
How do two people who really shouldn't get on end up in a relationship? Find out in this deliciously ordinary romance.

Return to Me by Erin O'Reilly
Will Salvation bring just that to Ellie, allowing her to find peace and happiness again, or will it have her questioning all that she believes in? A wonderful romance cloaked within an intriguing mystery.

Arc Over Time by Jen Silver
Book 2 of the Starling Hill Trilogy. This wonderful romantic continuation with the characters from *Starting Over* ties up loose ends. But the question is—does everyone have a happy ending? A must read.

The Presence by Charlene Neal
Can Rebecca and Kayleigh overcome ghosts from the past and their own insecurities, or will a presence from the past tear them apart?

A Walk Away by Lacey Schmidt
Sometimes chance brings you to the right person to help you resolve some of your baggage, and you learn to like yourself a little more. Kat and Rand are smart enough to recognize this chance in each other, but they also find that there is a catch to every opportunity—walking toward something is always walking away from something else.

Possessing Morgan by Erica Lawson
The investigation has barely begun when Andrea becomes the target of a nearly fatal hit-and-run. But was it really aimed at her? Can she and Morgan find the common ground they need to solve the case and stop the attacks, or are the gaps just too wide to bridge?

Twenty-three Miles by Renee MacKenzie
This is a story about community, and how it comes together in dangerous and devastating times. When you don't know who to trust, you better have friends who will rally around you. Will Talia and Shay find the answers they need to the mystery of the murders on the parkway, or will justice be elusive? Will they survive their quest for the truth?

Reece's Star by TJ Vertigo
Under Faith's guiding, loving hand, will Reece successfully traverse the rocky road of emotion and embrace the positive changes in her life? Or will she panic and be unable to control that Animal part of herself? Will she take that next step to declare herself fully capable of love and devotion? This third installment in the popular series that began with *Private Dancer* continues the passionate and often hilarious romance of Reece and Faith as they both grow in love and in trust.

The Chronicles of Ratha: Book 2 A Lion Among the Lambs by Erica Lawson
Can Jordana believe in herself like her Noorthi sisters do? Only then can she fulfill her destiny as The Chosen One.

Follow the colorful cast of characters in this action-packed adventure sequel as they traverse the galaxy. Of course, nothing ever goes smoothly when Jordana is involved.

Starting Over by Jen Silver
Book 1 of the Starling Hill Trilogy. There's a mystery afoot—whose royal resting place is disturbed at Starling Hill? All is revealed in this classic romance of simmering passions, anguished loss, and the wonder of love.

If I Were a Boy by Erin O'Reilly
Will Katie and Helen be able to make a life together work or succumb to doubts and the pressures of family? This story will fill you with the thrill of passion and the tenderness of love.

Terminal Event by Ali Spooner
Will the killer be caught or continue to evade authorities? Can Tally and Blair's budding romance survive the possibility? Read this intense murder mystery romance and find out.

Love Forever, Live Forever by Annette Mori
Fate intervenes and puts Nicky directly back into the path of her first love, Sara, and the corresponding events send her into a tailspin. Now she must decide—who will be the person she ends up living with and loving forever?

The One by JM Dragon

2015 GCLS Winner for Romance, Intrigue, and Adventure. The One is a romance with everything, love, intrigue, misunderstandings with a happy conclusion—the only question—who gets the girl?

Confined Spaces by Renee MacKenzie
Corporate politics, complicated romance, and long distances conspire to keep Andie and Kara all boxed in. Can love triumph despite the Confined Spaces?

Reflected Passion by Erica Lawson
Through a mirror, Françoise embraces life anew, while for Dale it is a powerful awakening, forcing her to discover not only her sensual nature, but the inner strength she possesses.

Flight by Renee Mackenzie
Some lives will be lost and others changed forever when the sisters' lives intersect. Will they be consumed by the wreckage, or will they be able to pick themselves up and take flight?

Cowgirl Up by Ali Spooner
Ride along with the MC2, for boot scootin', butt kickin', dirt eatin', rodeo adventures, with a love story thrown into the mix.

Printed in Great Britain
by Amazon

80235556R00159

E-Books, Print, Free e-books

Visit our website for more publications available online.

www.affinityebooks.com

Published by Affinity E-Book Press NZ LTD
Canterbury, New Zealand

Registered Company 2517228